Summit
Books

LÁZÁR

NELIO BIEDERMANN

TRANSLATED FROM THE GERMAN BY JAMIE BULLOCH

SUMMIT BOOKS

NEW YORK AMSTERDAM/ANTWERP LONDON TORONTO

SYDNEY/MELBOURNE NEW DELHI

Summit Books
An Imprint of Simon & Schuster, LLC
1230 Avenue of the Americas
New York, NY 10020

Originally published in Germany in 2025 by Rowohlt Berlin Verlag GmbH, Berlin as *Lázár*

Previously published in Great Britain in 2026 by MacLehose Press, an imprint of Quercus

First Summit Books hardcover edition April 2026

Interior design by Carly Loman

Manufactured in the United States of America

1 3 5 7 9 10 8 6 4 2

Library of Congress Control Number has been applied for.

ISBN 978-1-6682-0055-1
ISBN 978-1-6682-0057-5 (ebook)

For my family

CONTENTS

A blond poet perhaps goes mad.

—ALFRED LICHTENSTEIN

THE GLASS CHILD

I.

The snow of the dying century still lay on the edge of the dark forest when Lajos von Lázár, the translucent child with water-blue eyes, first glimpsed the man he would believe to be his father for his whole life and beyond.

It was the evening of Epiphany. The forest swallowed the last of the murky blue light. The room where the child was born lay in the western wing of the manor house, right next to the one painted blue, which nobody ever entered.

While the midwife washed the child's back, Sándor von Lázár stood at the window, scanning the forest. It was as if he had seen something vanish into the undergrowth.

He was standing there, feeling the cold of the glass, sweeping the edge of the forest with his gaze, letting it wander across the bark of the tree trunks, when a sudden fissure opened up inside him. At once he felt that well-known anxiety, the familiar panic, course through his body, flooding everything. Then he blinked and the fissure closed. He breathed a sigh of relief. He was not like his brother, nor like his mother, just slightly unsettled, which should come as no surprise given that his wife had just given birth to a baby whose tiny organs were visible beneath its transparent skin.

The baron ate dinner only in the company of his six-year-old daughter, who was not at all happy about the birth of her brother. When Ida, the German nanny, had taken Ilona to the room in the western wing, the girl had narrowed her brown eyes, looked very serious as she stared at this wrinkled, pale-blue, and bloated creature, and said drily, "He's very ugly."

Then she had hurried over to her father, who, unsure as to why she looked so wan, had left the window closed, and she had vomited on his shiny leather shoes and brown-checked trousers.

Now, after the baron had changed his clothes, the two of them were sitting at the dining table that was long enough to serve twenty guests a suckling pig, a goose, a pheasant, and three hares. They said nothing because they were used to Mária making the conversation. She was lying in soft satin pillows in the western wing, the child pressed to her breast, listening to his short breaths, Imre's constant clearing of his throat in the room next door, and the sounds of the house, feeling that she was sinking into the pillows, as if the pockets of her dark-blue cardigan were filled with heavy stones, whose weight was pulling her down, ever deeper, as she disappeared into the covers, mattress, and goose feathers. It was not a bad feeling, not a frantic falling or a panicked drowning, such as she knew from her dreams; it was a simple immersion, a silent receding from life; it was all she wanted.

Ilona could tell that her father was still angry with her by the energetic way he was cutting up his red meat. She knew he could sense her eyes on him—he could tell at once when someone was looking at him—but she could not avert them from the thick, bushy moustache that danced above his chewing mouth.

When her father looked up, she immediately turned her gaze to her huge plate. She did not understand how anybody could put such a coarse chunk of meat on such a beautiful plate of the most exquisite Herend porcelain, decorated with filigree butterflies, dragonflies, birds, and hazel twigs. Fortunately the chandelier was not lit, but the gas lamps on the papered walls showed more than enough. The trick was to focus on the golden upper rim of the plate, so it looked as if your eyes were on the food, whereas only at the bottom of your field of vision could you actually see what you were cutting up.

She heard her father chewing and, without looking up, knew he was allowing his eyes to roam the room. He was proud of all these possessions, although even young Ilona knew that he had nothing to do with any of it and that they owed their wealth to the people staring down at them from the paintings, who never gave the merest hint of a smile despite the many jokes they were told.

After dinner, Sándor moved to the adjoining smoking room, lit a cigar, and for a while paced up and down in silence. So far he had blocked out all thought of the newborn child, but now that he was alone, he could no longer fight against it. He smoked, frowned deeply, and thought hard, without being able to say what he was thinking about.

Török, the country doctor, was equally astonished by the child:

"I have to say, in all my years as a doctor I've never seen anything like this, my dear Baron. But the child appears to be healthy, its organs are functioning, and although the skin is extremely thin, it's holding up. Sunlight might be a danger to him, though."

So the child was healthy, which did not make the situation any easier. A stillbirth would have been simple.

At the thought of the next few years of his life, which would be determined by a see-through child, for the briefest moment Sándor considered lifting the baby from its mother's breast, putting a hand over its nose and mouth in the bathroom, and then replacing it on Mária's chest. This would allow him to continue living the life he was accustomed to, which he had arranged so as to maintain old traditions and create new ones, on a large scale as well as small, through the sedate progress of the years as well as in the convoluted haste of daily life. Already as a child he could not wait to tackle day-to-day business with the same solemnity as his father—

Pressing the dark-green signet ring into the red wax. Signing contracts. Receiving business associates. Pulling the pocket watch from his jacket. Raising the wineglass to his lips.

Following his father's example, the baron conducted his life according to strict routine. He got up at sunrise, pushed the pine-green curtains aside so his wife would wake up too (he could not abide late sleepers), went into the bathroom to shave his cheeks, chin, and neck, rubbed olive oil into his moustache, and then got dressed in front of Mária's puffy eyes, to show her how efficient, well-groomed, and superior he was. Then he would go down to the dining room to read the newspaper.

Mária did not get out of bed until she heard her husband's footsteps fade away in the hall. In the blue-tiled bathroom, she too picked up the razor, its handle still warm, and, with precise movements honed over the years, made small cuts in the soft, porcelain undersides of her arms, cuts so fine that there was hardly any blood and the wounds would close again after a few days. What remained was a barely visible patten of threadlike rosy scars that nobody ever noticed apart from Pál.

The young groom saw them when, one unusually warm spring afternoon, he helped the baroness up onto her white horse and passed her the reins. The sleeves of Mária's light-blue blouse had ridden up, exposing her forearm. She could tell at once from Pál's water-blue eyes that he had seen the scars; for a moment he was even going to touch her forearm with his coarse hand, but then he merely said, "Why do you do that, most noble Baroness?"

Mária had looked at the boy sympathetically, as if he were the one with the scarred arms, and then replied, "So I know I'm still alive."

When Pál helped the baroness out of the saddle that evening, he was just as sad as he had been three hours earlier. Mária felt as if she had not seen this boy properly before. She gave him a tender smile;

he turned bright red and hurried into the stable with the saddle. But Mária followed the groom, marvelling at his broad shoulders, and when she was just a few paces behind him she cleared her throat almost silently.

Nine months later Lajos was born.

2.

Two and a half years passed before the Baron looked at the boy properly for the first time and asked his wife the question she had been dreading for so long. Contrary to what she had expected, the fear had not subsided over the weeks, months, and years that had passed since the birth, but increased, for the question would come, this was certain, and with every minute the lie grew, driving its root system deeper into the ground, extending its leaf canopy farther and farther until it would overshadow her family, the manor house, and her entire life.

But Mária didn't allow her fear and the creeping lie to get her down. On the contrary, she resolved to face up to the falsehood, whet her knives, and sharpen her senses for the day when the question hovering over them all threatened to burst it.

For this, Mária had to learn how to lie. Her mother was a pious Christian who only wore grey and read the Bible for three hours every day—one before breakfast, one before lunch, and a final hour before supper. Throughout her entire life no untruth had ever passed her thin, bright-pink lips, and she had raised her six children to the same standards. If they did happen to lie and were found out, they were made to write out the Lord's Prayer one hundred times, with their left hand and using the oldest pen, without smudging a single letter.

And so it is all the more astonishing that Mária mastered the craft with such speed, consistency, and refinement. The method she used was as simple as it was successful: she lied whenever she could. She gave a false answer to each question she was asked, even if it was as banal as whether she would prefer to have paprika chicken or game for dinner. And with every lie that left her lips, she cast off part of her childhood self, left part of that Lord's Prayer–writing girl behind, gaining instead in self-assurance, shrewdness, and mischief, so that when Sándor finally posed the question she had been dreading for so long, she knew that her fear was unfounded, for by now she found it easier to lie than to tell the truth.

The question arose when the von Lázár family was sitting around the dining table, eating goulash soup. Mária was regaling them with a fanciful story, pretending it was the truth, while the others listened in silence, their thoughts elsewhere. Sándor was just wondering where love had gone when his son threw a chunk of beef at his chest. Looking up in disbelief, the baron saw his son sitting in the highchair, and for a moment did not know who this young person was.

He sat there, his snow-white shirt spattered with reddish-brown sauce, a scrap of beef over his heart, and could not say who this child was. Although the baron knew that the little boy was of significance to his life, he could not think why. Now, free from any preconceptions, for the first time he saw Lajos as he really was: blond, blue-eyed, and jellyfish-skinned.

Once more it struck him: this was supposed to be his son. But he did not look like him one bit.

"Are you sure that child is mine?" he asked as a joke, but aware too that he was terrified of the answer. Mária, who had played out this scene in her head a thousand times, said casually, "But of course, darling. How else would he look so much like Hayo the First?"

This was a bold answer, for there was neither a picture nor a description of the forefather of the Lázár dynasty, who at the age of fourteen had followed the Danube to Budapest with nothing save for a blue-black raven on his shoulder and a hunk of hard bread in a bag, had trained to be a jeweller, fought in the Siege of Szigetvár, surviving the battle thanks to his extraordinary cowardice, and then, to counter his innate solitude, had fathered sixteen children.

This mattered not, though, for as soon as Mária had given her answer, the baron sketched his own portrait, using Lajos as his model. And he was so delighted that his son resembled the famous Hayo that he completely forgot to give the child a box on the ear.

At first Mária was worried that the question would return, but it did not. Sometimes Sándor had the subtle feeling that he recognised the water-blue eyes or blond hair from somewhere, but Pál had died a few weeks after the child's birth, having been kicked by a horse, and so he merely hovered in the periphery of the baron's mind as a lost memory.

After Pál's death, the baroness did not leave her room for six weeks. This was not a conscious decision, a wake, or a prolonged moment of silence, nor a flu or persistent migraine as Sándor, who had not hesitated to move into one of the guest rooms, thought. No, she simply had not been able to get out of bed. All day long she just lay there, staring at the ceiling. Sometimes she cried, and sometimes she fell asleep with exhaustion, dreaming of the water-blue eyes she could have swum in, and feeling as she had with Pál when, after they had made love in the farthest stall and were still lying naked beside each other in the hay, he had run his rough fingers down her narrow spine and said, "I could snap this so easily. Like a dry twig. It would be the simplest thing because then I could have one half and your husband the other."

On the seventh day after his death, she got up and carried on from where she had left off. And yet she did not appear to find her way back entirely, because she could not rid herself of the habit of talking to the dead Pál, or of the bags under her eyes that had formed over the six sleepless nights. It was not surprising, therefore, that Sándor began to think of his mother and brother with increasing panic.

His mother who, following his father's death, kept running into the forest that surrounded the house, whispering muddled words to herself. This forest that had swallowed up his father while hunting. This forest that had spat out a dead stag instead. This forest that had hung a garland of ivy around the stag's antlers and put a fly agaric in its mouth. This forest that let the stag run until it collapsed outside the music room with its large windows. This forest that sent his mother signs. This forest that called her. This forest that snatched her. This forest that had swallowed his father, killed his mother, and driven his brother mad.

His brother. A man in his thirties who had been an intelligent, reclusive child, who had collected dead butterflies and beetles, watched birds, and drawn plants. His obsession with the natural world had come to an abrupt end with the death of his father. All of a sudden the expanse of the forest was a dark threat rather than a promise of freedom. All of a sudden he was afraid, afraid of the shadows that the boughs of the trees cast into his room, of the ferns that grazed his ankles, and of the birds that called out to him from the forest's depths.

One evening, when Imre went up to his room after dinner, he found a man sitting on his bed. He was dressed like a hunter and sat there, without moving, in the twilight, only his green, feline eyes darting back and forth in his dark face. When Imre lit a lamp, the man vanished; on the bedside table lay a book with the title *Night Pieces*.

3.

IMRE DEVOURED *NIGHT PIECES*.

He read it for the first time in the night of that day, which later would weigh as heavily and imposingly in his life as a large, lichen-covered boulder that diverts the stream of time in a different direction.

He tried to banish the image of the hunter, drew the curtains, and lay fully dressed on his bed. It was so dark that he could not see his own body; for a short while he was unsure whether he even existed. Through the ceiling he heard his mother, heard her talking and talking, about herself and the cook, whom she did not trust, who she always insinuated was stealing food and giving it to the poor children and widows in the village; about him and his brother, who was less handsome, but smarter and stronger-willed, and who would provide the better heir; about the pearl necklace that she never took off and yet was permanently looking for; and about the foaling horse, her portrait, and the painter with whom she had cheated on their father, which she now regretted more than anything in her life. All these words, this whole stream of dammed-up phrases, flowed down to him through the ceiling, disgorging over him, soaking into his clothes, his skin, and his bones until he seemed to consist only of this liquid despair, these watery feelings of guilt, and this fluid madness. Even though it was his mother who was speaking to his father; none of this was anything to do with him, was it? But how could you separate it, how could he fail to hear these words when he was of the same flesh and blood as them, the missing man and the grieving wife, who sat all day long in silence and as still as a stone by the window, gazing into the forest with crazed eyes that slid off the bark of every trunk, unable to find purchase on any leaf, scurrying like an animal from tree to tree? It was impossible.

The first night piece was a story by the name of "The Sandman." Imre read it in one go in the light of the gas lamp that stood on the small table by his bed. When he put the book down beside the lamp, he realised that his hand was trembling, that his arm too was moving about restlessly, and finally that his whole body was shaking. Fixing his gaze on the black cover of the book, he waited for the attack to subside.

Then he lay there still again. His mother had gone to bed. He heard his organs—heart, stomach, intestines—heard them working away, keeping him alive, realised how he was dependent on their functioning. He remembered—

He remembered the Grimms' fairy tales that Johanna, their Austrian nanny, used to tell them, and which superficially were not much different from the story he had just read. For this reason it had felt as if the tale was one of those he had fallen asleep to as a child and which he had not thought about in years.

The thing was, Hoffmann's story was disguised as a simple fairy tale, but in fact it was profoundly psychological and, without his being able to say why, an immeasurable comfort for him. Did he see himself in the sensitive, wildly imaginative Nathanael? Perhaps. Although it felt rather as if the story had burrowed into the dark pit of his stomach and uncovered something whose existence he had always known about, but which he was now seeing before him for the first time.

After his frantic breathing had calmed, he extinguished the light and tried to sleep. In vain.

He lit the lamp again, sat up, stuffed the pillow behind his back, and read the next story—and the next one—and the next. And so it went on until he had read the cycle to the end. In his overwhelming tiredness the individual stories strung together into a dark volume, with nothing separating them. The characters emerged from their milieus, meeting and greeting one another: the lawyer Coppelius shook the hand of Court Counsellor Reutlinger, and Ignaz Denner slashed open the chest of the narrator Theodor. When Imre's eyes finally closed, it was *he* whose chest was slashed open and, to make the matter more complicated, he was also the one wielding the knife.

To begin with Imre said nothing about the book and only read it at night, but it gradually crept its way into his daily life. For example, a few days after it had come into Imre's possession, it lay for all to see on the ottoman in the study, even though he was certain he had not read the book in there.

Soon he brought the tales to the light of day himself, reading one after breakfast, one after lunch, and one after dinner, over and over again. Now the book could no longer fail to come to the attention of Sándor, whose protective instinct for his puny, dreamy elder brother had turned into contempt since the disappearance of their father. For now, *Imre* was the master of the house; now *he* had to uphold the family's honour and transact business. But instead he gorged on horror stories and trash novellas, such trivial literature, diabolical tales and ghost stories, and was gradually losing his mind.

At first it was barely noticeable. Even though he would not stop talking about this book, at least he was no longer so withdrawn. And could he really be criticised because he preferred reading to attending to the family's affairs? After all, he was almost a child still, and unlike Sándor had never shown an interest in the fishponds, livestock breeding, wheat fields, and wood business. Even when he appeared at breakfast one morning sporting two different cuffs and a tie knotted wrongly, nobody was surprised—was it not understandable for him to feel shattered by the death of his father, whose body had still not been found? It was only when he failed to appear for dinner one evening that Sándor realised his brother's sanity was crumbling before their eyes.

He had just started on his soup when Béla, the butler, who had been sent to fetch Imre, returned to the table, saying that his brother was talking to somebody in the drawing room and had not reacted to his knocking. Sándor stopped short. Who might he be talking to? They did not have guests, and Imre generally avoided the servants, whose polite, almost sycophantic manner he could not cope with. Resting the spoon on the edge of his plate, Sándor stood up and said, "Excuse me, Mother, I'll be right back." Then he followed Béla to the drawing room.

Already from the hallway he could hear Imre talking to somebody. He sounded incensed, and he did not stop even when Sándor pounded his fist against the door. Who on earth was that? After hammering at the door once more, Sándor went in. With his back to them, Imre seemed not to have noticed that anyone had come in. He was wearing neither shoes nor socks and was wandering between the English hunting scenes and family portraits, gesticulating wildly. There was nobody else in the room.

Soon after that, Sándor took over the business affairs. His brother was sent to recuperate in a sanatorium in the Swiss Alps. He stayed there for six months, returned with a venereal disease and yellow eyes, took a spartan room in the western wing, which was painted blue to calm his nerves, and spent many hours a day staring at the forest. There, between the densely packed trees, he saw the characters from Hoffmann's tales. Sometimes his mother too, who went into the forest every day to look for the father's hunting lodge, which did not exist and never had. Until one day she never came back.

4.

There was no portrait or photograph of Imre. Not in any archive, antiquarian bookshop, or photograph album, not on any bedside table or chest of drawers.

If the photographer came from Pécs to take pictures of the parents with their spruced-up children, Mária on her white horse, Sándor and his friends after hunting, rifles over their shoulders and the slain red stag on the grass before them, or the manor house with its garden laid out in the English style, he would be locked away in the blue room to avoid his appearing by accident in the background. And yet, with his slender face, straight nose, and amber eyes, he would have made a good model, probably a better one than Sándor, in whom the aristocratic manifested itself in the way he spoke, ate, and dressed, things he had had to learn and which sometimes, in moments of absent-mindedness or tension, he forgot, leaving his entire aura to crumple. Imre, who appeared noble from his facial features to his hands, could by contrast wander barefoot through the garden and still look thoroughbred.

Sometimes Mária dreamed that her husband carried her naked, saddled, and on all fours into his brother's blue room, where she tied him to one of the bedposts and made him watch Imre and her make love. In reality she had exchanged scarcely more than a few words with her brother-in-law, for their lives ran in parallel. Her room was in the eastern wing and he only ever left his to eat. But he did not even eat with them, on the one hand because Sándor despised him for his illness, which he regarded as a weakness and a case of surrendering to his fate, and on the other because they regularly entertained guests from whom the dark side of the family was kept secret by every means.

Nor was Lajos allowed to eat at the long table until he could use his knife and fork flawlessly, and so he had to eat with his uncle and Ida the nanny in the small drawing room, for his parents would never have left him on his own with the madman.

And yet during meals a sort of friendship developed between the two. Lajos liked the man with the nimble hands that were continually on the move, never still, always stroking the seam of the tablecloth, the rim of the wineglass, and the tips of the knives as if they had to feel the ends of everything, compulsively; he had liked him at least since the day when, with a wink, Imre popped a golden-brown fried potato into his bowl of slimy semolina pudding.

The semolina pudding he was given day in, day out, in the belief back then that there was nothing better for children, was the worst thing he could imagine in his early childhood. Every morning, every lunchtime, and every evening he wondered what he had done to deserve this, and he was constantly thinking of new ways to please his parents. Would they like him better if he stepped only on the black marble tiles in the entrance hall? Or was he being punished because he cleared his throat too seldom? Or sang too often when it was raining? He could not work it out; the world of grown-ups was too complex and opaque.

Only Imre seemed to understand him. Besides, he was kind to him in a way that nobody else ever was, for whenever Ida looked out of the window, Imre would shovel some of his food into his nephew's bowl. Then he told these marvellous stories, featuring all the creatures and figures that Lajos sometimes encountered at the edge of the forest.

Ilona was envious of Lajos's being allowed to eat his semolina pudding in the little drawing room. Not only because whenever she ate offal, she could not help thinking of the cook's fleshy hands rummaging about in the dark, bloody belly of the animal, and of the fat, shiny bluebottles that landed on the hunks of meat, but also because she could not bear grown-ups. She did not understand how people could approach life with such indifference, how you could simply allow yourself to be rolled over by the years until one day the wheels were so heavy that they crushed you to death. Her father was the worst, with his painful seriousness, his deliberate movements, and his scrupulous decorum, which to him was more important than anything else.

Of course she found the other grown-ups ludicrous too, for example Dr. Török, who was probably the silliest person in the world. But in contrast to her father, the doctor was a likeable man because he seemed to be conscious of his peculiarities. Well aware of the healing power of comedy, whenever he was called to the bed of a sick child, he would waggle his large, sticking-out ears.

The cook too, who with her huge bottom could not fit through the door of the icehouse, or the groom, who always bowed deeply and theatrically, and said, "I hope you have a capital day, Baroness," when he ran into her—she found both of them ridiculous in this likeable way. She could not stand her father, on the other hand.

When Lajos was finally allowed to sit at the long table with twenty-four chairs, the backs of which were decorated with the family's coat of arms, he understood at once why Ilona had always envied him. Mealtimes were torture. All the while he was terrified of dropping the silver cutlery, for he was sure his father would then leap to his feet and drag him by the wrists into the next room to give him a thrashing while the dismayed guests continued eating in silence.

5.

The buzzing of a bee trapped between slatted shutter and window. Narrow strips of light slanting into the room and coming to rest on the flowery blanket, the Persian carpet, the pompous, dark furniture, and the yellow wallpaper. Thus the day began.

Opening her eyes, Ilona saw the yellow light coming into her room very differently from how it did in the manor house, and realised that it was spring.

At home she had difficulty getting up in the morning and thought that almost nothing could be worse than the shrill ringing of the alarm clock, which first bored into her dreams, then violently wrenched her from them. But here, in Héviz, where there was no alarm, only the buzzing of the bee and at most the pealing of the bells, she liked to get up.

Nor, upon rising here, did she have to face her father, who needed do nothing more than rustle his newspaper to put her in a foul mood for Mrs. Major's lessons. No, here she got up, went barefoot to the window, delighting in the parquet floor which felt so different from back home, and pulled up the roller shutters. In the manor house this was Ida's job and usually the last means of getting her out of bed.

Ilona opened the window. The bee flew off through the green branches of the chestnut tree. In the street, passersby, carriages, and vegetable sellers with wooden carts got out of the way of the automobile that Mr. Fehér drove up and down the avenue, as he did every Saturday. Ilona crawled back under the covers.

She loved lying in a warm bed with the window open, the fresh morning air, the dew on the leaves, and smelling the flowery blanket that had been washed with the same soap ever since she could remember. But what she liked most of all was hearing the sounds in the street that drifted into her room without disturbing the peace.

Whenever she lay in bed like this, everything was like the year before. And outside in the avenue nothing had changed since she had lain down again; she knew this without having to look, for she heard the rattling engine of Mr. Fehér's automobile, the sound of horses' hooves on cobbles, the cries of the fruit and vegetable sellers, and the high-pitched, happy voices of the women. This thought, that all of that existed quite independently of her, that this small world outside the window was still there when she was not looking at it, reassured her like no other.

But the weeks in Héviz were the loveliest time of the year not just for Ilona. Mária too blossomed in the spa town, not so much owing to the relaxing effect of the thermal lake, where the water was at body temperature, but chiefly because she was amongst people. Seeing and being seen was her restorative treatment, the gaze of others the only cure for that sense of not really existing, of being a mere construct of words and thoughts.

Here in the town she never had this feeling. Only sometimes, when she saw a particularly white cloud or came across an unfamiliar word in the newspaper, did she think about it, but in the way one thinks about a familiar pain which in retrospect is merely a vague memory. The idea that all of this—the newspaper she was reading, the chair she was sitting in, the reading glasses she was wearing, or the sky in which the cloud floated—was nothing more than a linguistic creation seemed so crazy that she shook her head, grinning.

Mostly she had no time for such thoughts, for the Easter ceremonies took up every free minute. You had to pray continually, eat, look for red-painted eggs, and pretend you had seen the Easter Bunny disappear behind the cherry tree or hibiscus hedge.

The weeks that followed were no less full of activity. During the day she tried to recover from the strains of the feast days in the warm water of the lake, although she kept meeting acquaintances with whom she had to gossip about other acquaintances; in the evenings they were invited to dinners or minor balls, or they visited the casino, open-air theatre, or a film screening. The opportunities were endless; the world, which shrank in the manor house, opened up again before her here.

When the yellow room was filled with the fragrance of the chestnut trees, Ilona heard through the wall separating her bedroom from the dining room the faint clatter of crockery, which always made her think of an oriental belly-dancer with countless golden bracelets on her narrow wrists. How easy it was on a morning like this to dream of the most magical places, given that here one could scarcely breathe in the face of such beauty! For it was spring, the deep, dark forest was far away, and in the town the trees were mere ornamentation. Here the chestnuts lined the main street in rank and file; only in the mornings and evenings did they rock their deep-green crowns, in full leaf, where the turtledoves sat and cooed. Sometimes Mr. Fehér in his automobile or a horse-drawn carriage would trundle along the bumpy cobbled avenue and then the top hats of the coachmen dressed in black would almost brush the lowest branches of the trees. And above all this was the sky—endlessly, unbelievably blue.

When the clock in the hall struck nine, Ilona got out of bed, closed the window, and, behind a screen, removed her nightdress and put on an embroidered dress. When she got to the table, Ida was removing the cloches from the last of the dishes.

Ida's body too was full of spring, even though to outsiders it looked as though a winter virus were raging inside her, for her cheeks were glowing red, her brow was burning hot, her eyes glistening feverishly, and her hands trembled as she put the platters and bowls on the table.

"Are you not feeling well, my child?" Mária asked her before every meal.

To which her husband answered, before the nanny could open her mouth. "Of course she's well! How could she be anything else with us?"

It was morning, then it was evening, and time raced in between because, with all the hustle and bustle, as well as the sunshine, one altogether forgot to take note of its passing. Thus the hours—days—weeks slipped past.

The father never stayed for longer than six days, after which he would leave to devote his attention to business again and check that everything was in order at the manor house. The time without him was even lovelier, for only then were they able to laugh—even at the table. Moreover, the good Ida was allowed to let her Paul in at night, when the children were asleep, and take him to her room, for the baroness knew what it was like when spring and fever raged inside the body and one could not find a quiet place to resolve the battle.

Only, the children were not asleep when the Grünfelds' long-serving domestic knocked at the door of the red-brick house late in the evening. Or at least not both of them. Every night, thirteen-year-old Ilona waited with aching tension and fervent anticipation for the heavy footsteps of the unknown man in the stairwell, because the muffled, rhythmic clacking and the stifled animal noises that reached her shortly afterwards through the ceiling produced an inexplicable tingling in her belly, which felt like the premonition of something great, important, and for which, strangely, the only thing that helped was a pillow wedged between the thighs, against which she could rub her belly.

Early in the morning, before the chestnut trees rocked their dark-green crowns, Paul had to go. He dressed, gave the sleeping Ida a kiss on her hot brow, left the red-brick building, crossed the deserted street, and entered the Grünfelds' house. In the boughs of the chestnuts the first turtledoves cooed, and Mária, who had been woken by the heavy footsteps on the stairs, thought of her Pál—and Ida, who had been awoken by the kiss on her brow, thought of her Paul.

6.

Jakub Jakubowski's best years lay far behind him (if they had ever existed in the first place). He had spent four decades on the easternmost border of the powerful Monarchy, on the doorstep of fertile and yellow Ukraine, as a captain's scribe. His life had been as monotonous as the landscape was expansive, the days barely distinguishable from one another. As the idea that the Habsburg Empire could be finite was inconceivable, there was not much to do—they were just one of the thousand small towns on the secured border of the huge imperium. The soldiers drilled, cleaned their rifles, boots, and swords, visited the casino in the evenings and then the brothel. Sometimes they would look up at the infinite sky or at the endless yellow solitude of the Ukraine and curse the emperor for his megalomania.

Jakub Jakubowski saw the sky and the landscape only in summer, for he entered the writing room next to the captain's study early in the morning and did not leave it again until late in the evening. In the intervening hours he wrote letters.

These were exclusively love letters, which he wrote in the captain's name to his seven girlfriends and wives scattered throughout the Monarchy. He also read the missives they sent back to the captain, and so after a short while he too had the feeling that he was loved by seven women in the empire. At the same time he became increasingly soft and less soldierlike, because daily contact with love smooths any edges.

Yet even here, at the edge of the world, time passes, and Jakub the scribe grew older. His hair turned grey, then white, and his hands restless. Eventually the captain was forced to dismiss him, because the smudged ink and jittery letters were at odds with the honourable, steely man he purported to be. Having belonged to it all his life, at once Jakub Jakubowski was no longer part of the imperial army, no longer a cog in this gigantic machine. From now on he was a simple subject, a short, old, Galician man, all alone in the endless expanse of the world.

No sooner had he arrived in the village where the manor house stood than he was unable to say how he had got there. The only thing he remembered was why he had opted for this destination. The why was called Judika.

Judika had been Jakub's favourite of the seven women. Just the sight of her neat, rounded handwriting made his heart beat faster. It seemed as if her handwriting contained her whole being, as if the letters were a reflection of her appearance, her thoughts, and her world. She described this world in such detail that the streets, houses, and trees in the village felt familiar, as if he had been living there for years himself.

He could not recall how he had imagined it would play out, but certainly not as it did. Wiping his sweaty hands on his jacket, taking a handkerchief from his inside pocket, wiping the sweat from his brow, putting it back, and removing his hat, he knocked at the door and waited. Nothing happened, so he knocked again. After a while, a door opened on the other side of the street. A woman with a blue apron around her tummy and a half-plucked chicken in her hand called out, "You'll be waiting a long time. Judika is dead."

When Lajos was five, Sándor hired the former scribe as a tutor, without knowing that the man had spent his whole life writing nothing but love letters. After briefly considering that he too must die, Jakub had bought Judika's house and all her furniture.

The baron gave him strict orders not to be too soft with the boy, not to go easy on him, and certainly not to shy away from the cane or military-style instruction. The boy was to learn what it meant to be a man, a baron, a von Lázár.

But Lajos soon realised that the gentle Jakubowski would never beat him. In any event he did not give him cause to. He was a diligent pupil and a fast learner. What he loved most of all was writing. Although "love" was actually the wrong word, for he did not write out of love, but out of a compulsion that felt totally natural, a compulsion best compared to that of having to breathe. The boy felt as if he had to write down everything of importance, as if things would slip from his grasp otherwise, as if they only achieved their legitimacy by his setting them down in material form.

And so it came to pass that Lajos noted the foundations of his world, the most important events, on various pieces of paper. Most of these went missing without his being able to say where. When he asked Imre about this, his uncle said, "The house swallows them. It lives off memories."

But one memory from 1906, which unlike the others was written on expensive letter paper, turned up again somewhere decades later, as if not even the house could take it away from him.

GHOSTS

7.

THE YEARS CAME AND WENT, MOVING LIKE THE ROMA WITH their circus wagons and horses through the Habsburg Empire, through the Monarchy as it sank into the Danube swamp. And on their way through this old empire, ruled by an equally old emperor-king, on their spiral journey through the fields and forests and towns, down to the future bones, into the blood-red depths of this young century, the rambling years did not spare the Lázárs' family house either.

The children became older, Mária lonelier, and Sándor more aloof. He now travelled more frequently than in the past to Pécs, which for him had always been more of a distant, painful memory than a city. In Pécs he had loved properly for the first and only time! How could he wander through the streets there without thinking of when he and she had once walked beneath these trees, shoulder to shoulder? How could he stroll through the park without recalling that she and he had sat on the green benches, shoulder to shoulder?

It was impossible. He had been unable to forget her, not in the manor house and certainly not in Pécs. At the end of every street he saw her turn the corner, he saw her sitting in every coffee house, and each time he forgot that she was no longer here. He found it incomprehensible that people could just disappear, that they died and disappeared, and it was as if they had never existed. For dust thou art, and unto dust shalt thou return.

And yet he had seen often enough how life withdrew from the body and how the body slipped from the world of the living into that of the dead. So often that he was permanently afraid it would soon happen again, soon another person would vanish from their life, and the phantom pain would afflict him again.

Sometimes, out of the blue, he found himself back outside the hospital without being able to say how he had got there. Then he would stand outside the large building and look through the branches of the lindens that lined the street, up at that blue window from which, many years earlier, he had looked through their branches down to the street. At the time he was still a child, a child who had been sent to the city to study agricultural sciences. But he had not cried. Now he was a man and the child long dead, but every time he stood here, beneath the lindens and the blue window, tears came to his eyes.

It was—had been—impossible for Sándor not to grieve in Pécs. For the years had come and gone, and their circus wagons had trundled along the cobbles of this city too; their horses' hooves had also echoed through the streets of Pécs. And amidst all the nationalism, anti-Semitism, thirst for flesh, and hunger for blood which they had brought with them, there had been some love too, which had fallen at Sándor's feet, of all the people in this city, even though he was here only briefly and on business.

The whole thing had occurred on the square outside the mosque with its green-blue dome from the time of the Ottoman occupation. There a woman had walked past him whom he had never seen before and yet he followed her, for beneath the turned-up collar of her coat he had spotted a small mole that had deeply touched him. The sudden thought that the tiny brown blemish made this inconspicuous woman different from every other woman in this world made him forget his business appointment and follow her flowing coat.

The woman strode through the open square in front of the mosque like a deer crossing a large clearing: quickly, tense, and without turning around. But as soon as she had turned into one of the streets, she went so slowly, as if she never wanted to reach the end of it. She walked so slowly and the large white clouds, which the wind drove across the steel-blue sky, moved so quickly overhead that Sándor had the impression he was standing still. But ahead of him he heard the persistent, rhythmic clacking of her plain button-up ankle boots.

And so they wandered the length of the autumnal city whose facades gleamed in the October sun and whose trees blazed red and yellow, until the woman stopped outside an austere-looking house in the workers' quarter at the edge of the city. In the street it smelled of dead leaves and urine, and an old, wrinkled face peered out of every third window of the sooty workers' houses. Sándor felt the listless gazes on his back, and, as he approached the woman beneath the bare plane trees, their trunks like sick bodies dotted with growths, he was more conscious than ever of what his handmade brogues, his tailored trousers, his Algerian camel-hair coat, and his Viennese hat had cost.

When he got to the front door, the woman, whose every movement was carried out with unbelievable care, was still standing there. The old men peering out of the windows propped up on their elbows saw the noble gentleman with the black hat and good shoes give a curt bow to Mrs. Virág and essay a smile. Then they saw the gentleman say something—quite a lot, in fact, for his mouth moved for a long time, mechanically, as if it were its own small machine. And then Mrs. Virág entered the gloomy stairwell, followed by the distinguished gentleman, at which a husky murmur went through the street, stirring up the dry leaves.

After finding love again, the baron travelled to Pécs for a few days every week. He told Mária and the children that he had important business there requiring his utmost care and attention; after all, the business was critical in determining the circumstances in which their descendants would live. Mária, who ever since Lajos's birth had been a champion liar, saw through her husband at once, of course. But she was too worn out to broach the matter, too tired to add another battle to the many minor ones they fought on a daily basis. There were too many fronts already and her exhaustion was so stifling and heavy, it was as if she had trudged for hours through cold rain and was now sitting wrapped in thick blankets by the sizzling fire. She felt that she had given up, only she did not know what.

And so once a week the baron paid for a hotel that he set foot in only to collect and return the key. The rest of the time he spent in Mrs. Virág's tiny flat, which he had not hesitated to purchase for her. He had also bought her new clothes and button-up ankle boots with pearls in the heels, and every time he left he placed such a large pile of pocket money under her pillow that she gave up her job at the lace factory.

But she did not love him for the money! She loved him for his elegance which, despite the immense effort it cost to keep the mask in place, came across as perfectly natural. Even in her humble flat each of his movements was of such extraordinary beauty; even when, like the old men, he peered out of the window, smoking his Russian cigarettes, and the air smelled of burning wood and urine, he was the epitome of elegance.

Despite this, he was not above sinking his face into her seldom-washed loins. On the contrary, he idolised her body, which she regarded as ordinary at best. But perhaps this was precisely what Sándor was looking for: a body that was nothing but a body. For Mária's body was no longer just a body but a symbol. It had become the ruined temple of a long-forgotten religion, whereas Mrs. Virág's body was the site of a blossoming faith, at which Sándor regularly worshipped by thrusting into her wet loins, licking the dirt from the soles of her feet, burying his nose into her armpits, and placing her buttocks onto his face.

Beneath these he was able to forget everything: the poor grain harvest; the national aspirations of the Balkan lands; Russia breathing menacingly at their backs; the great emperor-king who, small and old, reigned over his crumbling realm; his brother; his wife; and even his weak, pale son.

8.

When Sándor pushed aside the pine-green curtains and opened the window, Mária knew that the starlings would gather today. She could already hear the birds individually in the trees of the grounds. Through the open double door to the bathroom she could see her husband's back as he shaved over the sink in his vest.

The cold morning air that poured into the bedroom through the window smelled of chestnut trees and dark needles. Mária pulled the blanket up to just beneath her chin and thought how the starlings would soon be in Rome or North Africa or elsewhere in the Mediterranean. She longed for the sea and was anxious about the coming winter, which was galloping towards her from the north-east like a wild horseman with an icy sword. If she closed her eyes, she could see the hooves of his white horse crashing on the hard, frozen ground and hear the ice tinkling in his thick beard. How she would love to be a starling, escaping the winter!

Sándor left the bathroom and got dressed as he gazed out of the window. She knew he did this only to avoid having to look at her; he had no feeling for anything. For him a tree was just a woody plant, a human being merely an intelligent animal, and a story nothing more than a fiction. In the past, around the time of their wedding, Mária had clung to this simplicity. Sándor and country life had given her a psychological stability that had been unthinkable in her parents' dilapidated villa and at the girls' boarding school. The social decline of her family and of Viennese society with all its pretensions, codes, and rules, with its decadence and double morality, and the endless balls that were evenings in hell for Mária, had been too much of a burden for her. Her marriage to Sándor had been her liberation from all of this. But now, after all these years, his simplicity and the monotony of rural life had lost their charm.

Pushing up his tie knot, Sándor turned away from the window and looked at her. As he did every morning, he narrowed his eyes slightly, took his golden watch from his jacket, and said, "Business is calling. And you, my dear, ought to get up too. The children need you."

With a thin smile he left. Mária listened to his energetic footsteps fade, then got up and went into the bathroom to cut her arms. The burning pain and the sight of the thin red trickles on the white porcelain of the sink gave her strength. Then, under running water, she washed her blood from the blade and put it back in exactly the same spot where her husband had left it.

Meanwhile Ilona awoke from childish dreams, in which she had encountered woodland creatures that talked and singing trees, with a small dark-red stain between her legs. She got a fright but did not scream or cry. Instead she got up, instinctively threw the cover over the stain, as if she needed to feel ashamed at having soiled the beautiful white linen, and gave her body a thorough inspection. But she could not see any wound. She did not feel any pain either, at most a slight tugging in her lower abdomen. But she had hardly eaten anything the day before, because with great skill she had manoeuvred every one of the revolting grilled kidneys, which she thought tasted only of urine, into the large dark-red napkin in her lap and from there into the mouths of the three dachshunds beneath the table. This is what she usually did when served meat, for the thought of eating something that had once had eyes made it come right up again. She decided to forget the stain.

When she entered the dining room, her father was already sitting at the table, reading yesterday's paper. It had travelled a long way here by train, for the baron read only the *Budapesti Hírlap*. He believed that as lord of his estate he needed to know more about world affairs than the people who lived, worked, and reproduced on it. This was why, rather than reading the local rag, he took the newspaper from the capital, as a result of which he was better informed than all the others, but later too, for the paper only arrived at the manor house in the afternoon. As it was inconceivable for him not to embark on the newspaper at breakfast, his reading was delayed by a whole day. And thus the world he learned about always belonged to the past.

So that he could not watch her out of the corner of his eye while reading, Ilona sat opposite him, spread dark-yellow honey on her bread, and hoped that her mother would come soon to wipe away the silence.

After breakfast, Ilona went up to the round tower room where lessons took place. She was mainly taught by Mrs. Major. With Mr. Jakubowski she only had German and empire studies; his way of speaking and his view of the Monarchy were distorted by all those years at the frontier. Although his speech followed the rules of German grammar, it was studded with so many foreign words that it would barely have been understood in Vienna. As far as his view of the emperor and the Monarchy was concerned, it was that of somebody who had spent a long time abroad. He spoke about the emperor as if he were still a young man and the empire as if it had not changed over the last forty years. Like Sándor he lived in the past—but for some people there is no other place.

Mrs. Major was the tutor for housekeeping, mathematics, and Latin, although nobody really knew if she was fluent in the language of the Romans. Neither Sándor nor Mária had ever learned Latin, but the baron, who regarded the Habsburg Monarchy as the modern incarnation of that vast, glittering empire, thought it essential that his children did.

When Ilona entered the tower room, Mrs. Major was standing beside the tall clock, listening to its reliable ticking. Ilona did not know why the "Majoress," as she and Lajos called her, always stood here, but from this ticking, or more generally from the passing of time, she seemed to draw her strength for the whole day, like Mária from her daily pain.

The clock struck the top of the hour, and Mrs. Major began at once—and without a word of greeting—to initiate Ilona into the secrets of a respectable household. She paced watchfully up and down in front of her pupil like a real major before his soldiers, all the while slipping the hard ruler from one claw hand into the other. Ilona tried to imagine her as a child, without success. The woman was like an ageless witch, who was fluent in the language of the Romans presumably because she herself had been alive back then.

The lesson refused to end, and Ilona's concentration leaped from Mrs. Major's severe silvery-grey bun to the insistent ticking of the clock, and via Jakub Jakubowski's voice, which droned through the ceiling, to the sounds of the starlings—but the one thing it avoided altogether was the Latin text about the end of the Roman Empire. Eventually, this lesson was succeeded by another, and so it went on until the morning was over.

The von Lázár family often took lunch without the father. On that day, however, he was already at the table when Ilona entered the dining room. As soon as she saw him sitting there at the head of the table, flanked by his wife and son, she became aware of her stomach ache again. She sat beside her father, feeling the eyes of her forefathers gazing down at her stiffly from their portraits. How she hated these people! Their stony faces, their extravagant hairstyles and repulsive sideburns, their black eyes, red cheeks, thin lips, white hands, and ridiculous clothes. How could they look down at her so patronisingly? Had their lives, plagued by rotting death, diarrhoea, and illness, not taught them otherwise? No wonder the young baroness was so thin, for how could she not lose her appetite under the permanent watch of her ancestors?

But now she had to eat—Ida brought the dishes in. And she was lucky, for there was very little meat and heaps of vegetables: shimmering purple beets, deep-green spinach, cheerfully bright salad, gleaming white horseradish, yellow potatoes swimming in melted butter, and luminous carrots amongst funny little peas. She shovelled decent portions of these onto her gold-rimmed plate and began eating, without listening to her father's mechanical chewing, her mother's lies, or her brother's nervous swallowing. Ignoring and suppressing things was one of her greatest gifts, for unlike her mother and brother, who were dreadfully affected by the whole world, like a tortoise she was able to crawl back into herself, deep into a place where nobody could reach her.

After lunch, Ilona went to see the horses, who always made her forget her unbearable family. She brushed their shining coats and stroked their warm necks until she felt cold. On the way back to the house she heard something rustling in the rosebushes. Then a faint whimper.

Out of curiosity she went over to the edge of the forest and thought of the injured fawn that her father and his brother had found in the field when they were children and brought back to the house. Maybe that something whimpering amongst the rosehips was a fawn too.

When she was only a few paces from the spot, the creature ran away in panic, and Ilona, desperate for a fawn of her own, followed it excitedly into the forest, though she had seen nothing but a few twigs quivering and leaves trembling.

The dense, brown foliage is already in the trees. But the dust of summer still glistens in the breeze. The starlings dart straight through, astonishing the world anew.

Ilona hastens as if out hunting game. A tree trunk, an eye, a leaf, a grave. She hurries and sees, taking nothing in.

Her feet follow invisible paths. Narrow, shadowy tracks. Dug by animals into the fabric of the forest.

Lost, she rushes through yonder gate. The walls rise up high and straight. Silently enclosing the unknown city.

The daughters crouch in their thorny lair. The king enthroned in the undergrowth. And impassively the creatures stare.

Through the leaves a strange wind does creep. The elms sing and whisper. For the dead child they weep.

The entire village stopped work to search for the baron's daughter. Silently and obediently they combed his expansive fields and dense forests. The hounds had been given the young baroness's sheet as a scent; nobody had said a word about the bloodstain.

Late that afternoon black clouds gathered. Imre, whom Sándor visited for the first time in years in his blue room, to ask if he had seen anything, talked of dark ships, collapse, and of a great war.

Meanwhile Mária, gasping for air in panic, stood in the garden and watched the starlings rise shrieking from the trees and hover above the house as a large, black, swirling cloud.

9.

It was already getting dark when a peasant found the baroness unconscious in the forest. She was lying, fragile and small, on a bed of moss, as if a giant had gently laid her there. Her white dress was torn, her lips were blue, and there was dried blood on her thighs. Pavlović, as the peasant was called, carried Ilona out of the dark forest, just as many years earlier he had carried his wife over the threshold into his dark house. His daughter looked so battered that the baron thought the peasant had raped her. But what could he do? He paid the man a finder's reward to the value of thirty chickens, and the peasant's rough brown hands closed tightly around the golden crowns.

Ilona was laid in her freshly made bed. Sándor lent Dénes, the groom, his beloved black horse so he could fetch Dr. Török to the house as quickly as possible. But even the doctor was at a loss.

"I have to confess, most noble Baron, that I'm afraid there's little I can say about your daughter's condition. She appears to have suffered a great shock, and I believe, or in fact I'm certain, as certain, at least, as an old country doctor like me can be, that she's battling hypothermia. I think there is nothing more we can do except to give her a hot-water bottle and allow her to sleep. There's no better medicine than that. And as for the blood on her thighs, I can reassure you, my dear Baron. Your daughter is now a woman; that's all there is to it."

The doctor left the house and rode back to the village. The parents were worried. Like two guards they sat at the head and foot of the bed in which their daughter lay and said not a word to each other. The light from the hall slanted into the room through the door, which was ajar, dividing Mária and Sándor from each other. And so each of them remained alone with their own anxiety.

* * *

Ilona slept for twenty-six hours. Then she awoke with such a raging appetite for meat that she devoured half a chicken and an entire platter of kidneys. She could no longer detect the faintest aftertaste of urine, for which she had loathed these kidneys; now it seemed to her as if she had never eaten anything so delicious before.

When Ilona had finished wolfing, she wiped her greasy hands on the topmost of the many blankets and said, "I dreamed of a world that was covered in grilled meat."

Deeply embarrassed, her parents could manage no more than a hint of a smile. What were they to do if their daughter dreamed the dreams of simple, hungry peasants?

"We're delighted you're feeling better again," Mária said. "We were terribly worried about you."

Ilona waited—for so long that Mária wanted to fill the silence with a lie—then said, "It was wartime and the meat was dead people."

For several weeks it was as if Ilona had come through a second birth; she was as helpless as a newborn baby, cried a lot and at every opportunity, and could not remember anything. Even the peasants in the village, to whom Dr. Török had to give a detailed report of her well-being after every visit to the house, were concerned. The doctor was at a loss. All he could do was repeat that he had never come across a case like this before.

Gradually, however, Ilona's memory returned, came back home to her like a soldier believed dead. To begin with nothing changed as the images were restored, such a stealthy process that Ilona herself barely noticed it. Although the occasional fragment of memory flashed in her mind, at first the images were so disjointed that she thought nothing of them. Time passed and more memories came back, which Ilona carried around silently.

When she had finally found the words, she sat in front of the crackling fire and told them what she had salvaged from the ruins of her memory of that day. It was no surprise that it had taken her so long to be able to talk about it, for the language she spoke in was not her mother tongue, which was full of symbols and metaphors, linguistic gems and verbal flourishes. This might be appropriate for talking about a time which lay so far in the past that it could no longer be dangerous, but not for one that was breathing down her neck like her ancestors.

Ilona had had to develop a narrative language of her own which was so simple and clear that she could not become entangled in it. But her parents were so disturbed by this direct way of talking, which led them straight and without warning into the dark, bare heart of the forest, that they did not believe a word she said. Although they comforted her and promised to send hunters into the forest to kill the "creature," Ilona could see the lies on their faces—even on her mother's.

Ilona sobbed and raged, ate the chicken wings, duck legs, hare livers, cured beef, veal schnitzel, kidneys, and sausages with her bare hands, and clutched in such desperation to Ida's skirt when she came to put out the light that Ida had no choice but to lie down beside the young baroness's feverish body and wait for the restive sleep.

The winter came and went, and the parents had to accept that their family happiness at the manor house was at an end. When a friend of the baron's put a quarter of his fortune on the wrong horse, Sándor bought one of the man's smaller mansions from him, in a sleepy little town, and Mária, Ida, and the children moved into it in the spring. He stayed behind, which bothered neither him nor Mária. They pretended it did, of course, out of decorum towards each other and consideration for the children, but in fact both of them were happy with the way things had turned out.

10.

He had a Roman nose, an intelligent chin, sad eyes, and long, powerful fingers which, whenever she glimpsed them, sent a shudder down Mária's body. The young man went by the name of Jonathan, and he was Ilona and Lajos's new tutor. Like the family, he was also a newcomer to the sleepy little town. He had moved from Vienna, which he had left on account of its decadence. The excess of prostitutes, automobiles, parades, picture houses, beggars, cats, officials, and political viewpoints had struck him as unhealthy, and the immorality in which the city dwellers lived highly questionable. He longed for a simple life in a rural town. He would have loved to have been a peasant or a farmhand, but, as he knew, his fingers were only good for writing and amorous endeavours. In these disciplines they were outstanding, for no other hands in the whole of Vienna had written such beautiful poetry and brought so many women to orgasm.

The young man had no interest in the poems, which he sold, gave away, or burned. The orgasms, on the other hand, were noted down with great care and scrupulousness in a fat little book that he always kept with him. Sometimes he felt as if he were carrying around in his book not merely the names of these women, but their souls too.

Ilona could not evade him either. One glance at him had been enough to make her bones vibrate. She could not even say what had fascinated her—the morning light spilling onto him through the watery-green crowns of the trees, the deep green of the small lake he had wandered up and down, or just the man himself, his way of wandering through all this green and gazing out at the island in the middle of the pond.

* * *

When she met him for the first time, she was convinced that this was what it must feel like: to die.

He came through the door—and the room was changed in an instant. Everything became important the moment his eyes fell on it, and the idea that a tiny part of him and her consisted of the same memories and experiences seemed utterly unbelievable.

While Jonathan stood by the blackboard, telling her about the wanderings of Odysseus, she hung on his every word without understanding a single one. In any case, what mattered to her were not the words, but the movements of his lips, which she could have watched all day long. But this lesson too was eventually succeeded by another, and so it went on until the morning was over.

Far too quickly.

For after lunch, which the young teacher always took with them, he retired to contemplate the relationship between nature and modernity. Then he walked through the garden like a sleepwalker, and it almost broke her heart to think that he barely noticed her. To him she was no more than a child. And not even that, she was a vessel, a vessel of wet clay that he could shape and fill as he wished.

Yes, he could shape and fill her as he wished, but he, who kept a book on the hundreds of women he had brought to orgasm, had no intention of dragging her innocence through the dirt and adding her name to his list.

This, despite the fact that she did everything to excite his imagination and would have given anything to lose her innocence in the dirt, in the rosebed beneath the window of the schoolroom, for example.

Jonathan, on the other hand, wanted a simple life. He wanted to teach in the mornings and wander through his thoughts in the afternoons. He wanted to watch the roses grow in the garden and study the flight of the swallows. He wanted to sit in the sun and the shade and listen to the song of the cicadas.

And Mária? Mária pined for water-blue eyes, blond hair, powerful shoulders, a broad neck, and strong arms. Jonathan was gangly, with dark hair and brown eyes. But when her gaze fell on his long, strong fingers, her belly began to tingle; it stopped only when she wedged a pillow between her thighs.

She could not remember when she had last slept with a man. It must have been several years earlier in Héviz—they had slept with each other sometimes there. Sándor and she. But afterwards she had always felt ashamed, as if she had been raped, not by him but by her own lust, against which she was defenceless in the dark.

Meanwhile the baron enjoyed his, but especially Mrs. Virág's, lust, to the fullest. He had not left the bed in days. The air in the room was stale, the sheets stained. By now he knew Mrs. Virág's moles better than his own; her body was as familiar as his estate. Conscientiousness and lust had fought an epic battle in Sándor's head, from which the latter had ultimately emerged as the bloodied victor. And so Sándor forgot his business, his family, his manor house, and his forest, drowning instead in Mrs. Virág's warm skin.

II.

When Jonathan had been living with the Lázárs for three months, without properly taking notice of Mária and Ilona, who fluttered around him like moths around a light, he had a momentous dream—

He dreamed that he awoke
Woken by the night bells
Striking midnight
He stepped to the window
Saw the moon
Saw the garden
Saw the pond

The frogs were quiet
The water spirits silent
The water sounded
Darkly soft around Mária's legs
Who came in
Her skin of porcelain
Her hair of glass
Her eyes of crystal

The water enveloped her
As if she were returning
Her naked body
Vanished into the darkness
White like the moon

And stepped forth unfleshed
Onto the island

The following morning, when Jonathan was sitting opposite the baroness, he found it impossible not to imagine her as a bare skeleton. Later too, when he initiated Ilona and Lajos into the secrets of geometry, he was unable to banish from his mind the idea of Mária's empty ribcage, her pearl-white shoulder blades, her slender fingers, and her butterfly-shaped pelvis.

The dream raged inside him like a fever—for weeks on end. The only relief came from penning poems, which he wrote on yellow writing paper that he generously sprayed with his scent and left everywhere: in the rosebed, in the dining room, on the clock in the hall, beneath Mária's pillow, at the shore of the lake, even under the church pews. Soon the entire house smelled of Jonathan's scent. But it was Ilona rather than Mária who found the first poem, and she was certain that the words were meant for her. If in the past she had toyed with her few feminine charms, now she mobilised them for all-out conquest. Whenever possible she would go upstairs or downstairs in front of Jonathan, pulling up her dress so high that he could see her calves. In his presence she would also drop everything so she could brush his hand suggestively when he picked the items up and gave them to her.

One evening, emboldened by a particularly fervent poem she had found under the Persian carpet in the drawing room, Ilona lay in wait for the young teacher in the dark hallway and leaped on him with her flushed body, desperate for his lips and fingers.

The August evenings were blue. They lay in the fields like tired vagrants, settled on the grounds, beneath the weeping willow by the shore of the small lake, took a rest on the beds, the sofas, the thick carpets, and in the armchairs, as if they had a long journey behind them. As if they had come from far away, from a distant, forsaken realm. Even more forsaken than the foundering Monarchy.

On one of these evenings the baroness and the young teacher met between the poppy fields that surrounded the little town. Both had been waiting for the blue hour with longing, for the dusty bright days seemed inappropriate, tactless, barbaric even, in view of their aching hearts.

No sooner had the sun sunk behind the hills than Mária and Jonathan had left the house; she walked to the left around the town and he to the right. They had spotted each other from afar, for the summer sky still held the light of the day.

At first they wanted to turn around, for they had never come across each other outside before. But now that they had seen each other this was impossible, of course.

As they continued to approach each other, without knowing whether to look or not, they both grappled for words and the correct tone, quietly rehearsing various greetings to themselves and trying out topics of conversation—only to find themselves face-to-face, empty-mouthed. They were not able to manage even a "Good evening"; they merely gave each other panic-stricken stares, searching in vain for all the words they had just practised, and eventually began to laugh out loud.

Although they had never spoken about these things, Jonathan knew about Pál, and Mária about the hundreds of women in Jonathan's young life. The relationship between the two of them was one without words. With his fiery poems, which years later, when the manor house was in the hands of the Russians, still turned up in the strangest places, Jonathan appeared to have exhausted all the words allotted to him. But what were words? All that counted were feelings!

Around the same time the conversations between Mária and Ilona dried up too, for the glances between her mother and the teacher had not escaped the daughter's attention. Now she also understood who the poems had actually been written for, which meant her mother unknowingly became her rival. For unlike Ilona, who registered every gesture, every smile, and every look, she saw nothing anymore.

The father came at Christmas. He had to come at Christmas; even he knew this.

No sooner had he stepped down from the carriage than Ilona rushed at him with her broken heart and overflowing eyes, to tell him in her quavering voice about the alleged attempted rapes by the young tutor—"It was the beginning of winter, Father, but the days were already short. I was standing with my back to the window in the drawing room to read in the last of the light. The tutor then came in. A cold shudder ran down me for I had noticed the way he looked at me, that dark, stinging gaze. I mean, I saw him every day; every day I had to see him! And he actually came up to me and kissed me, kissed me, Father, kissed me right on the mouth! And I couldn't scream, couldn't hit, couldn't flee. All I could do was stand there, as if I were made of stone. He kissed me on the mouth, brow, neck, chest—and then he forcibly turned me around so my breathing fogged the window. Thank goodness there were footsteps in the hallway and he had to let go of me. But, Father, oh Father, I can still feel his breath on my neck!"

And, sobbing, she fell onto the baron's chest.

That same day the teacher went with his luggage between the wintry poppy fields to the station. Three days later a peasant found his body, frozen stiff, with ravens circling above. His face had been so badly battered it was unrecognisable.

12.

The Easter weeks of 1912 were the time of sleepless nights.

After Jonathan's murder, which without any investigation was blamed on the Roma living on the edge of the town, Mária slept for six days on end without anybody being able to wake her. And she had been unable to sleep ever since. Although she lay in bed and closed her eyes, this was only to preserve the semblance of normality. The half of the bed beside her was mostly empty, for the baron spent his nights in a simple hotel near the station, where he had installed Mrs. Virág. It was a puzzle to him how he could ever have lived without her. In the evenings he told Mária he was going to the casino to meet acquaintances and business associates; although she knew he was lying, she was not interested in the truth.

Directly beneath the roof of the narrow, three-storey brick house lay Ida's room. And directly beneath Paul lay Ida.

The animal noises of these two kept Ilona awake; she tried to satisfy her irrepressible desire into the early hours of the morning with a long white candle.

Only Lajos slept deeply and soundly.

Ever since he could think, he had had this one dream: huge ships putting out to a wide, dark sea, leaving the port where they had been born, forgetting their background. Until the day when he saw a photograph of the *Titanic* in the newspaper, cut it out, and placed it beneath his pillow, the ships had been archaic three-masted sailing vessels. But now he had seen the most modern ship in the world, whose four gigantic funnels darkened the sky and whose wake drew a foamy white path across the Atlantic. It was still only a dream, but in a few days it would become reality.

He had to ride out a week before his dream became reality. A week of masses and feasts for which they squeezed him into the most uncomfortable Sunday suit and almost strangled him with a tightly knotted tie. In other respects too, the Easter weeks were pure torture for Lajos. When he wandered through the busy streets, he sensed eyes on him; when he sat in church, he heard people whispering about him in the pews behind; and when he talked to people his own age at dinners, he was constantly asked if his grandfather had been Count Dracula.

In the evenings, when he lay in bed, he envied the peasant children in the village, who did not have to dress up and become stiff in order to live up to their parents' expectations, who did not bear surnames that needed to be honoured, who did not have ancestors who were immortalised in statues and paintings and had streets named after them. He wished for nothing more than to be able to change his skin, to shed it like a reptile.

While Lajos waited for the *Titanic*'s departure, he felt as if he himself would be on board when the time came. In his mind he was standing on deck, watching the hills of his mother country fade away, his paternal lighthouse shrink, and the island of his birth sink into the sea. Everything had to sink, submerge, drown so that he could finally be free, his own person at last, unattached, without the noble title on his finger, the history on his back, and the chain of ancestors around his neck.

When, one mild April evening, the baron hurried down the avenue with a newspaper beneath his arm, up the steps, and along the landing into Lajos's room, the son turned to him and said, "Are you not feeling well, Father?"

The baron, whose heart was still beating in his windpipe, replied, "Read this!" and threw the evening edition of the paper onto his son's desk.

Lajos read. Then he got up, closed the window, and sat back down. He stared past his father. Looked through the door. Saw the landing. Imagined cabins on either side of it. Imagined icy water up to his ankles—knees—chest. Imagined the house breaking into two, leaving nothing above him save for the night. Floating around him were sixteen hundred human bodies. On the seabed lay one hundred million marks of sunken jewellery.

Lajos got up, opened the window, and sat back down. The evenings still smelled of the incense from the Easter Masses. The *Titanic* had sunk. Nature had triumphed. The father stood in the bedroom. On his finger he wore the green signet ring. He stood behind Lajos's back and placed his hands on his shoulders.

Lajos felt as if he himself had drowned.

A day later, when his world was shattered to its fragile core for a second time, Lajos was still standing beside himself. He had slept beside himself too, in his own arms, for who else could have comforted him, who else understood his pain?

He walked in duplicate around the thermal lake too, over which dusk had settled. He saw its dark water, the trees that lined its shore and the lamps that lined the street, the wooden bathing house, and him walking beside himself. He did not see the fever circling him like a tiger, ready to yank him to the ground at the right moment and tear his flesh off. Its shoulder blades grinding, the tiger followed him through the twilight, prowling through the reeds and creeping up on him ever closer—until with a powerful leap it pounced.

He stood before her, not knowing where to look. She had the same unsettling gaze as she'd had six years earlier, when they had met on the avenue and then he had committed to paper the memory that the house kept spitting out. To avoid her gaze he focused on her blue teardrop earrings.

Before he could introduce himself, she said, "I like your skin. One might think you only leave the house at night."

Lajos smiled.

"My grandfather was Count Dracula."

She laughed!

"Nonsense! Count Dracula lived in the fifteenth century, and he wasn't a vampire. Just cruel in other ways," she said.

Lajos ventured an astonished look into her eyes.

"How do you know that?"

"My father told me. He's interested in folk tales and myths."

"All the same, you shouldn't go out walking on your own in the evenings."

"Accompany me, then," she said with a smile.

They walked once around the entire lake and then back along the avenue. She talked a lot about her mother, whom she could barely remember. The teardrop earrings had belonged to her too. Lajos felt ashamed, because surely it was better to have a mother who forced you into smart suits and into church, and suffocated you with a tie, than not to have one anymore.

When they were standing between their houses, he finally plucked up courage to ask her name.

"Lilly. What about you?"

"Lajos."

"Goodnight, Lajos."

"See you soon, Lilly."

But they did not see each other soon, for the following day Mr. Grünfeld had to leave prematurely on business—and Lilly had to go with him back to Vienna.

13.

SHE HAD DREAMED OF THEM, AND INDEED THE STORKS HAD returned, craning their white necks from the corn-poppy fields that surrounded the village, while she stood at the window, taking in the milky-blue morning sky, the blossom-yellow horizon, the soft hills in the distance, the simple church tower, and the rich red of the fields, as if everything were already a memory, as if seeing and remembering were one and the same; then she closed the window and went into the bathroom, where she washed her face, cleaned her teeth, and sat on the lavatory, sitting tight for a while, but she could only urinate, which left her with the unsatisfying feeling of having left something unfinished, but the white necks of the storks rose up from the red fields, which was why she left the bathroom without cutting her arms, went into the bedroom, spent a long time wondering what to put on, torn between the green dress and the blue one, eventually remaining in her nightdress, for now that she had begun to not finish things, she could continue in the same vein, and so she sat as she was at her dressing table, painted her lips corn-poppy red, put the pearl earrings that had once belonged to Sándor's mother through her piercings, loosened her braided hair, which glided like dark water over the white material of her nightdress and her narrow shoulders, stood up and fetched the dark-blue cardigan from the wardrobe, put it on, went out of the bedroom without glancing back or shutting the door, down the stairs to the first floor where the children were asleep, still asleep, for soon the good Ida would wake them and push the curtains aside to allow in the day, whose early hours would wipe from their faces the childishness they still inhabited while asleep, but now they were still lying peacefully and quietly, lying there as if dead, but the darkness smelling of milk and sleep was full of dreams that spanned the room like spiders' webs, which she brushed from her shoulders as she went down to the ground floor and left the house, stepping out into the blazing morning, kicking off her shoes, and walking barefoot across the grass, damp with dew, behind the building to collect the large stones that had fallen out of the wall and lay on the ground, and put them in the pockets of her cardigan, before wandering down to the pond, its smooth surface reflecting the green crowns of the trees and the sky, crossed only occasionally by a bird or broken by a fish leaping out of the water, until she took one step in, then another, until she felt her feet sinking into the muddy bottom and the weight of the stones in her cardigan pockets; until the water enveloped her as if she were returning.

DREAMS

14.

The baron only found out that they were at war the day after the imperial proclamation. As ever, he had not read the daily newspaper, which arrived from the capital in the afternoon, until the following morning. Even then he could hardly believe it, though it said at the top in thick black letters TO MY PEOPLES! and at the end stood the name of His Apostolic Majesty himself. The whisperings about war, which had become ever louder over the years, spreading across the globe like wildfire, telling of a conflict that would produce more heroes than the Trojan War, had not made their way through the dense forest that surrounded the house. Within these walls they still lived in a time in which a war was inconceivable, the end of the Monarchy unimaginable.

But not only did the baron live in the past; since Mária's death he had also been living alone. He had sent Mrs. Virág back to Pécs and the children to Catholic boarding schools in the genteel outer districts of Vienna. He had handed over the running of his businesses and estates to a young, ambitious businessman from Pécs, who regularly awarded himself handsome bonuses for his at best mediocre work, and without Sándor's knowledge. Sándor, meanwhile, spent his days drinking. Alcohol helped to combat the feeling that he was unable to cope with life, despite his barony and wealth, despite his strict routine of many years, his merino wool suits and silk ties. And it allowed him to stifle the grief over his late wife, whose death he had desired more than once, but whom now, as if in a tragic romantic film, he would cry over bitterly, kneeling beneath her portrait. How strange death was, and how easily it could turn a life upside down!

While her father groped his way drunkenly along the corridors of the house, drank Unicum as if it were water, and slept wherever the alcohol knocked him down, at boarding school Ilona now finally lived the life she had been craving for so long. The forest and its creatures had dwindled to no more than a vague memory, as indefinable as the perception between dream and reality. For the very first time she was surrounded by other girls; all of a sudden she could talk to her peers and ask without shame those things she had been desperate to know for years; now she could laugh and dream.

And how she dreamed! During the day and at night, but especially in the evening, after the nuns had gone from room to room and turned out the lights. Then the girls lay in their narrow beds and spoke into the darkness, confiding in her their innermost wishes and desires, their darkest secrets and most embarrassing experiences.

Lajos, on the other hand, did not enjoy boarding-school life. He felt like an outsider amongst these young men who turned everything into a duel and strode through the world as if they were made of tin, who constantly talked of the coming war from which they would one day return home victorious, and of women's curves.

Lajos often thought about women's bodies too, ever since he had woken up the previous winter with a damp sticky patch on his underwear. But he was sickened by the way his classmates talked about them. The war had made its way even into this domain. Women had to be "conquered" and "subjected," and their bodies had to be "stormed" like a battlefield, with the courage to "break all resistance."

A few weeks after his arrival, Lajos was spoken to by a boy he had not noticed before. He had short, chestnut-brown hair, sticking-out ears, and very small hands. They were so small that when the boy held out his right hand and introduced himself as Caspar, Lajos hardly dared shake it. He asked him if he had been at the boarding school for long.

"A fair while. But not for much longer now, thank goodness!" Caspar said. His voice reminded Lajos of a small, grey, heartless animal.

"Why not much longer?"

"Because the Fatherland's going to need us soon! My father says the war is already at the gates of Europe."

Lajos tried to imagine this, the war at the gates of Europe, but without success. He did not even have a clear idea of Europe; all he really knew was the Monarchy. He knew its borders and languages, its peoples and rivers, its mountains and battles. All these things that made up his country were part of him too, were part of his family and his history, a part of him without which he would not be conceivable. Europe was merely a word by comparison.

"How does your father know that the war's there?"

"He knows His Majesty, and His Majesty knows everything."

Lajos nodded. If the emperor was saying that, it must be true. Then the war actually was at the gates of Europe. He felt slightly scared, but did not let it show, nodding eagerly when Caspar asked him if he would like to come to the ruin too.

The ruin was a former chapel; its roof had caved in, and a walnut tree was growing in the middle. It stood on the edge of the property, casting its shadows over the stone wall onto the neighbouring pasture. Sheep grazed there in summer.

Caspar went ahead. He had very narrow, bony shoulders; Lajos would not have been surprised if he had no shadow. They did not talk, merely heard the twittering of the invisible birds and the crunching of the gravel beneath their shoes. The sound unsettled Lajos, giving him the feeling he was walking on armoured beetles.

Standing by the ruin, which was so thickly entwined with ivy that the stone beneath was no longer visible, were two other boys whose names Lajos did not know. One of the two was holding a long white candle. He was tall, blond, and had such a pronounced jaw that Lajos felt certain he would be able to bite through rock. The other had a flat, round face, small eyes, and bloody lips he kept chewing on.

The blond boy was called Melker, the other Balthasar.

Lajos was so amused by the candle that he could not help laughing. It seemed alien, out of place, like something the boy had purloined from another world and which was now upsetting the balance of this bright, warm May day.

"Why are you laughing?" Melker asked.

"Because of the candle. I've never seen anyone wandering through a garden in broad daylight with a candle."

"Oh, I see," Melker said, grinning. "It's for you."

15.

THE WEDDING WAS HEAVENLY AND TOOK PLACE IN THE SUMmer of the Battle of Verdun. The days were hot enough that they could still sit outside in the evenings, in the beautiful green nightfall, as the shells turned Verdun into a cratered landscape. The boys, who were barely older than Lajos, actually felt as if they were on an unfamiliar star, infinitely far from the world they knew. On average they survived at the front for fourteen days.

Fourteen days after the wedding, Ilona and Kurt were still not used to each other. After her time with the nuns, it felt strange living with a man. She had the impression that he belonged to a different species, and the Berlin apartment that was now their home did not feel like one at all. Both were fine, however, in the gathering dusk. As it had been back in her dormitory, the darkness was easy to talk in.

They talked a lot about the war, almost exclusively, as if it were the only topic of conversation they had been able to take along to their island of solitude. The war frightened Ilona. So much so that, ever since she had taken the decision to live with Kurt, she could no longer breathe properly. It felt to her as if Berlin were a city in the Himalayas, where the air is so thin you believe you are suffocating the whole time.

Kurt was a pacifist. He had only briefly been caught up in the general euphoria. Ilona too was against the war, but at the same time she despised Kurt for dodging military service. Partly because her husband shared her fear instead of countering it with something, and partly because she found men in blood-spattered uniforms unbelievably attractive. There was nothing that excited her more than the idea of subduing in bed a man who was fighting for bare survival, killing other men.

In bed she yielded half-heartedly to Kurt, almost grudgingly. And yet he had an inkling of the fantasies that lurked deep inside her, somewhere amongst her viscera, a place she did not even know herself. He had sensed them the very first time they met at the ball, when he had seen Ilona standing at the side, beneath the tall, dark window that reflected the spectacular chandelier.

She had dreamed of balls like this all her life, but now that she was able to attend them, they were as much of a torment for her as once they had been for her mother. It was in such moments, when she stood on her own at the side, watching the cream of Viennese society spinning in circles to the music, that she missed Mária the most. What she would have given to be able to escape these occasions and sit again in front of the fire in the manor house, listening to Mária talk about the adventures of Hayo Lázár!

She was deep in such thoughts when a young man approached and invited her to dance. Hold on! Not just any man, but young Kurt von Bleichröder, whose grandfather had been a private banker and friend of Bismarck! Was this possible? Was the grandson of the banker, who in his time had been one of the richest men on earth, asking her to dance? Yes, this was actually happening. Kurt had spotted her and known at once that she was the woman he was going to marry. She was beautiful, no question about that, but it was not the shiny dark hair, the slim pale neck, the small, shell-like ears, or the pointy nose that enthralled him. What mesmerised Kurt was the earthiness and mossiness that clung to her without his being able to say why. She was not dirty, nor did she have that sort of smell, but if he thought about her childhood he always imagined her living in the undergrowth of a thick, dark forest.

Six weeks after their first dance, they were married.

Lajos continued to suffer life at boarding school. He had not left the place since arriving there shortly after Mária's death, for he did not dare to return to the manor house in the summer holidays. He was convinced his father would be able to tell just by looking at him. Even though he slipped off to the washroom several times daily to scrub himself from head to toe with the coarse horsehair brush under icy water. Even though his skin was red and sore, and wearing his uniform had become agony. Even though he shaved his armpits and pubic hair every day.

During lessons he would daydream with glassy eyes. In his mind he tortured his classmates and teachers in every conceivable way. He crucified them and broke them on the wheel; he burned them on huge pyres, then, their skin bubbling with heat, threw them into ice-cold water; he flayed them, dribbled lemon juice onto their raw flesh, sprinkled it with salt, then fed them to the rats and ravens. Or he simply beheaded them, as his ancestors had done with the Ottomans.

In his sleep he cried so loudly that the others would wake and hold his pillow over his face until he lost consciousness. Then he was quiet.

Lajos could only breathe freely in the summer holidays when his fellow pupils went home and the school lay abandoned beneath the large sun. Then he spent the long days in the sprawling garden, thinking that transience was the greatest calamity, but that a world without it would be unbearable.

When he lay in the shade of one of the pear trees, though, listening to the chirping of the crickets, and saw the blue sky through the branches, he wished that time could lie down in the grass beside him and never have to move on. And when he gazed at the long blue beetles with the black blotches on their backs, he wished he could be part of nature like them. He wanted to be everything: a tree, a stalk, a river, a moon—just not a person anymore.

These were the things that Lajos thought about on those languid summer days. Then he would draw the blue beetles so that he could remember them in greater detail in the cold months of the year.

* * *

While Ilona was busy settling into her new life, the war continued to rage in Europe. Although she and Kurt discussed it, this was mainly because it was impersonal and so easy to talk about. The war was common property and a better topic of conversation than the weather.

But while they sat in the dusk and chatted about the war, neither could stop thinking about the things that were actually on their minds and the questions they dared not ask. How should they handle each other, sleep beside each other, eat in front of each other, and think of each other? And most important of all: how should they have sex with each other? Yes, this was the biggest question overshadowing everything else, even the war.

Ilona fell in love with Kurt one September evening in the penultimate year of the war. While the soldiers of the Great Army were suffering from hunger and exhaustion on all fronts and the German Empire was sending its youth out onto the battlefields in the uniforms of its dead, they sat reading in the drawing room, the balcony door open, Schumann's *Bird as Prophet* playing on the gramophone. Seeing them sitting opposite each other like that, both absorbed in their Schnitzler novellas, one might imagine they were one of those couples whose children had long flown the nest and whose relationship had been like that of siblings ever since. In actual fact they were both driven by the same sexual desires as Schnitzler's characters. Only, unlike the latter, they did not prowl through the night with their craving, but sat quietly together reading. This afforded them some relief at least and also provided a second topic of conversation. Although they did not dare use the admissions of the characters as an opportunity to air their own erotic fantasies and dreams, each of these conversations harboured a tension resulting solely from the knowledge that the other had also read those passages.

A shadow fell across the brightly lit room.

They both gave a start, and there was a cry of fear that Kurt attributed to his wife. Then he got up, as if meaning to catch the bat with both hands, which in view of the tall Jugendstil ceiling was of course impossible. But now that he stood there while Ilona still cowered, terrified, in her chair, he felt manly and strong—perhaps for the first time in her presence. He also knew what to do, how he could eviscerate her to finally lay open those hidden fantasies. He no longer cared about the bat fluttering nervously and disoriented around the stuccoed ceiling. Wrenching Ilona up by her hands, he clamped her under his arm like a tree stump and carried her into the bedroom. Then he threw her onto the marital bed, slipped off her dress and underskirts, and sank to his knees in his black suit, breathing heavily before her.

Ilona was shaking with excitement.

She slowly pushed her foot into Kurt's mouth and began to pleasure herself.

16.

As the war came to an end, so did Lajos's time at boarding school. He returned to the manor house where nobody was waiting for him except the ghosts, memories, and empty bottles.

As he made his way through the deserted rooms and corridors, he knew he would find his father lying somewhere, unwashed and unconscious or yellow and dead. All of a sudden he also knew how his father must have felt when he became master of the house far too early. Lajos wandered through the desolate house, gathering up all the bottles which the last remaining servant had long given up trying to battle. As he did this, Lajos got the impression that *his* father had died too.

But then he saw him lying there, the man he had been frightened of all his life, lying unconscious on the handwoven carpet, with his arms wrapped around his knees like a freezing, worried child. His face, though, was like that of an old man, traversed by thick veins and deep wrinkles. He must have been lying there for quite some time, for the vomit around him had already dried, its acrid stench filling the entire room.

Lajos put the bottles he was carrying on the floor next to his father. Then he squatted beside him and touched his shoulder. For a second he thought he might have been mistaken and that his father was actually dead. But then he saw he was breathing and shook his shoulder to wake him. It was a while before Sándor opened his eyes, as if his life had retreated deep into his inner core and, when he had finally sat up and said, "Hello, my boy," as if part of him still lay buried somewhere.

* * *

The feeling remained. Sándor, once such an elegant man that one always felt ashamed in his presence, was now a wreck. Already in the mornings he would be dragging himself drunkenly around the house, drinking his Unicum from a porcelain cup to keep up appearances and preserve his dignity. Yet it was precisely this clinging to the past, and the alcohol-soaked old version of himself, that obliterated any sort of dignity. But Lajos too struggled to detach himself from the image he had formed of his father when he was a child. He still found it impossible to contradict him, even when he babbled meaningless, drunken thoughts, or pinned the responsibility for Mária's death on Lajos and his sister.

Sometimes he was nagged by the feeling that his father was just playacting in order to test him or to pull the wool over his eyes for inexplicable reasons. But then he would find him once more beneath the piano or lying in a rosebed, with trousers damp at the crotch and cuts on his palms, which Lajos kept bandaging up.

Three weeks later the war came to an end with the downfall of the Habsburg Monarchy and the realisation of Gavrilo Princip's dream. After the assassination of Archduke Franz Ferdinand and his wife, Princip was chained up in a cramped, damp cell, alone and in total darkness. He tried to commit suicide several times—even after one of his arms had to be amputated because of his poor health—and scratched the following words on the wall with a spoon handle: *Our ghosts creep through Vienna, whispering in the palaces and making the lords tremble.* Sadly for him the young man did not get to see the end of the Monarchy he so despised, for his tuberculosis, of which he was aware at the time of the assassination, delivered him from his suffering seven months too soon.

For Lajos the end of the Monarchy was the only logical outcome; he had always regarded the physical and mental decay of his father as its embodiment. He even saw the death of the emperor two years earlier as a premature consequence of his father's disintegration. It felt as if everything were falling apart, as if the centre could not hold, as if he were part of a world that no longer existed.

One morning Béla found the young baron lying unconscious in the bathroom with an ashen face and a cut on the side of his head. Although Dr. Török, who was summoned, was as clueless as ever, he prescribed Lajos a five-week cure in Héviz.

As conscious of tradition as his father, Lajos stayed in the narrow brick house in the avenue of chestnut trees. At first he had been reluctant to follow the doctor's advice, but now that his sick father and the endless empty bottles were far away he was glad he had listened to him. It was as if he were not merely geographically distant from everything at the manor house, but he had also moved in time. He felt like the child once more who, with the newspaper photograph of the *Titanic* beneath his pillow, was dreaming of being at sea, of leaving everything behind him.

When, in his second week, a car stopped outside the house opposite and the driver opened the door for a young lady, his childhood fever returned too.

Although in the six years that they had not seen each other he had conducted make-believe conversations with her every evening, although in his imagination he had confided in her all his fears and concerns and believed he knew her better than any other person, he did not dare go over and invite her to take a walk. And yet it would have been so simple! He would not even have had to ask, for they had already made the arrangement six years earlier. That counted for nothing, of course. They had been children at the time, nothing but clueless, stupid children. She probably wouldn't remember who he was anymore. They had spoken only once; what did he expect? How many people did you speak to without remembering them? How many faces did you come across daily, especially in the streets of Vienna, and what was one that you had last seen before the war?

All the same, a flicker of hope remained.

In the third week Lajos awoke in the middle of the night in a red room full of dancing shadows. For a moment he thought he was dreaming, for since his fever had come on, he often dreamed he was running through burning forests. But when he went over to the window, saw the Grünfelds' house in flames, and the heat assailed him with a potency that would not be possible in a dream, he knew it was serious. He got dressed at once and ran outside to rush into the fire for Lilly Grünfeld.

Fortunately she was standing in the street at a safe distance, next to her father, who was staring at the flames in disbelief. In a moment of uncanny prescience he saw in them all the horrors that the near future would bring. He would not speak or eat for days.

By contrast Lilly and Lajos talked to each other animatedly, as if having to let out all the words that had dammed up over the past six years. Late into the night these words were still flowing through the thin wall that separated their beds. For after the fire Lilly and her father had found refuge in the empty rooms of the brick house, where the father of course had taken the parents' room and Lilly that of Lajos's sister.

While Mr. Grünfeld was trying to convince the authorities that the fire had been caused by communists who were planning revolution throughout Europe, Lajos's fever gradually subsided. At the beginning he was unable to be in the same room as Lilly without being plagued by a shortness of breath, difficulties swallowing, and outbreaks of sweat, but now he could talk to her face-to-face. And now, when he heard her singing in the next room, he only seldom passed out.

On the second Sunday in Advent Lajos awoke from a dream in which the armistice was merely a practical joke that the old despots had played on their citizens out of boredom. Amused, they exhumed the dead, put them in their blood-smeared uniforms again, and sent them back to the front with a handful of grenades.

When he woke up and heard, instead of the resounding laughter of those wielding power, Lilly singing *O Tannenbaum,* he quickly brushed his teeth, left his room, entered hers without knocking, and kissed her.

17.

The honeymoon got off to a good start. They had a railway carriage to themselves, the countryside that rolled past peacefully was vast and green, and their anticipation endless. Although the last few months had been wonderful and exciting, they had been strenuous too. Lilly and her father had lived in the brick house until the wedding because Mr. Grünfeld was still trying to convince the authorities to follow up on his suspicion of arson. He left the house in its burnt state as if to convey a message; in truth he simply did not have enough money to finance the rebuilding of it, for during the war nobody had been interested in the products manufactured in his lace factory.

While Mr. Grünfeld fought a tireless battle for justice and Lilly made sure that he still ate and slept from time to time, Lajos commuted between heaven and hell. Heaven was the brick house in Héviz, which he could no longer imagine without Lilly; hell the manor house where his father, like the ghosts, drifted around pale and thin between the bottles of alcohol.

Had someone told Lajos a few years earlier that one day he would miss the version of his father he feared and who despised him, he would never have believed it. But now that Sándor no longer resembled the man he was, neither outwardly nor in character, Lajos actually did wish for the old one back.

The feelings he had for his father swung between pity, disgust, love, and contempt. But Sándor too was the victim of intense mood swings. Sometimes, usually approaching lunchtime when his sick body, after a comatose night and crushing morning full of nausea and liver pain, slowly got into gear and his blood alcohol level was high, but not yet at the boundary of unconsciousness, he was almost like his past self. He would then curse Lajos for having allowed the house to fall into such disrepair and call him a failure, a disappointment, an unworthy, milky-skinned freak. In the afternoon his euphoria would be replaced by a profound sadness and despair, and he would cry uncontrollably.

The sobbing echoed through the house until the onset of dusk, and if the baron bumped into his son in these hours, he would fall to his knees, grab Lajos's hands with his sweaty ones, and entreat his son to forgive him for Mária's suicide and the denial of any paternal love.

After dinner, Sándor's emotional state changed once more: he drank deliberately to arrive at the moment of unconsciousness, shifted the blame for Mária's death onto Ilona and Lajos, and could no longer control his bodily excretions.

Outside the window stood a horse chestnut that was so large and had such thick foliage that it was gloomy in the young married couple's hotel room, even in the glorious June weather. Lilly and Lajos were not affected by this; on the contrary, the horse chestnut reminded them of the avenue in Héviz and the dim light in the room enhanced the feeling of togetherness they had been craving for so long. Besides, the scent of the cones of white flowers that almost hung over the bed when the window was open had been Lilly's favourite since childhood.

As soon as they arrived they had thrown open the shutters and fallen happily onto the double bed. She and Lajos in a room all of their own! She and Lajos and their love for each other, which would not have fitted even in the largest of their trunks! And this bed! Heavenly! One bed for the two of them and no wall separating them any longer! It was unbelievable! Yes, she was still unable to believe that they were actually married and allowed to do what married people did.

Before the wedding she had still been afraid of this, imagining the worst and longing for her mother as she had never done before. But when the time came, she soon realised that Lajos was no less uncertain than she. Indeed, to begin with he was so nervous he could not even get an erection. Only when Lilly—out of pity, affection, and relief that sex evidently had nothing to do with the scenes of torture that she had imagined the term implied—began to kiss his soft, squishy glans did Lajos's penis become hard and extremely large. But now that she had befriended it, not even its size frightened her any longer. Fearlessly she spread open her legs and took him inside her all the way. Since then she had not been able to get enough of him.

While Lilly opened the window Lajos hung up his coat and hat, removed his cuffs, and rolled up his sleeves; summer had already arrived in Zagreb. Then he went into the bathroom, washed his hands and face, then gazed into the mirror for a while. Through the open door he could hear the gentle rustling of the leaves and the fabric of Lilly's dress, and as he stood there in the bathroom, looking at himself in the mirror and thinking about their long journey, it felt as if his life had begun again, as if he had been born again right now, in this unfamiliar room in this unfamiliar city.

He had laid the foundation for this himself a few minutes earlier when omitting his noble title while signing the register at reception—at a stroke he was now merely Lajos Lázár.

Five hours later the baron, sitting alone at the dining table, took his dinner consisting principally of wine and cognac. It had been a warm day, but now it had cooled and started to drizzle despite the evening sun and clear sky. As ever the baron sat at the head of the table and because he had asked old Béla to open the window to let in the smell of the damp meadow, he felt a fine sprinkling of rain on his left shoulder. He did not like the pheasant, once his favourite dish, but the wine was excellent. Contrary to his habit of throwing alcoholic drinks down his throat like a man dying of thirst, he even went so far as to hold each sip in his mouth for a few moments.

The fragrance of the summer rain reminded Sándor of his childhood and his brother, for whom he suddenly felt profoundly sorry. He wanted to go over to the west wing and embrace him, but of course that was out of the question. One had to keep one's countenance, after all.

Instead he opened another bottle of wine, filled the crystal glass to the brim, and now did empty it in a few mouthfuls. Then he closed his eyes and held his napkin to his nose, to coax out the memories that came with the rain, but the gentle patter and the twitter of the birds carried them back to him.

It was unbearable and at the same time unbelievably lovely. He had forgotten that he too had once been a child; so much life lay between him and that time.

After finishing the newly opened bottle of wine, he sensed how the memories were sinking into the dark swamp that over the past few years had become more familiar to him than anything else. Now he felt steeled to tackle the pile of letters that lay beside the plate with the cold pheasant meat. He had promised Lajos to read the letters during his six-week absence and answer any urgent ones—"preferably when you haven't drunk so much," his son had said, forgetting once more which of them was the father. But Sándor did not want to think of Lajos's impertinence now; the swampy indifference surrounding him was too lovely.

Having no letter opener to hand, he took instead the greasy meat knife. There were six letters, none of them requiring an answer, and yet the last of them preoccupied him for a long while. It consisted of two sheets of yellow paper that had arrived in a blue envelope, both blank. There was nothing written on the envelope either.

After Sándor had inspected it carefully, he put the letter in the breast pocket of his waistcoat so he could look at it again in the morning, with sober eyes. Then he got up, swaying only faintly, to sleep in a bed again for the first time in many nights. As he climbed the stairs, he tried to remember the route the young married couple were taking. Now they were in Zagreb; from there they would go to the coast and Trieste, then on to Venice and via Verona to Florence and Rome. Yes, he said to himself, that's right. Then, to his surprise, he thought how pleased he would be to get a postcard from them.

That was when he tottered slightly, missed the top of the last stair, kicked the riser, lost his balance, and fell backwards all eighteen stairs to the bottom.

Contrary to the assumption that one's whole life flashes past, in Sándor's mind there was only the image of a single person as, his skull broken, he waited to die of his brain haemorrhage: the young groom with the water-blue eyes.

18.

THE VERY NEXT MORNING, THEIR FIRST ABROAD, THE HOTEL manager personally brought them the telegram with notification of the death. And so the young Lázárs' honeymoon ended before they had seen the sea. Obviously they were disappointed, but also relieved that on their return they would not have to share the house with Sándor.

After the funeral, which was thoroughly depressing, Lajos swore to honour the name Lázár with deeds rather than by merely assuming the baronial title. The first thing he did was to provide the peasants with new fertiliser to improve yields. Then he revived relationships with the family's business associates, which had withered under his father. But the most important step he took was to invest in the internal combustion engine factory in Pécs, which had sprung up almost overnight and reduced the unemployment rate in Mrs. Virág's area by half.

Lajos's impression of being reborn in the hotel bathroom was not wrong, for in fact he was no longer the man he had been a few months earlier. All of a sudden he was a businessman, which was strange because in this role he felt close to his father for the first time. At a stroke the distance that had existed between them all his life was gone. Finally he understood that there had been love somewhere, hidden beneath an armour of strictness and discipline.

Sometimes Lajos would wake in the morning with the feeling of being his father before Sándor had begun to founder, for his life was now ordered in a way he would never have believed possible. Since the first time he glimpsed himself in the mirror, he had been certain he would have to get away at some point. He had never seen himself with a wife, as a baron, or as someone who gave banquets. But that was precisely what he was now doing.

The manor house, whose guest rooms had accommodated nothing but spiders and ghosts for so many years, was once more a place where people conversed, danced, and laughed. Lajos felt as if he had been transplanted back into the golden era of his grandmother, who had lived so extravagantly that she had her personal dairy cow transported by train to wherever she went. The only difference was that now it was not just nobility sitting around the table, but impressionist painters next to countesses and priests next to fiddlers, whose haunting folk melodies brought tears even to the eyes of the lieutenants. And always amongst them sat Imre, silent, his gaze sunken in the forest, but nonetheless happy to be there.

11 August, 1919

Dear Ilona

I am still very sorry that you could not be at father's funeral, not so much for his sake, but more because we have not spoken properly in far too long. Since the wedding I have often wondered how your marriage is, how you live and speak together. Is it not strange that we are of the same blood and yet know so little of each other? If you feel like it, please tell me about your life. For the time being I will, unsolicited, tell you something of mine.

Lilly is settling well into the manor house. She likes the countryside here and takes pleasure in riding. It is nice to fill the house with new memories, but I have to admit I am sometimes still unsure how to live with a woman; much time has passed since we lived in the town with our mother. But I shall get used to it. Business is going well; the factory's turnover is increasing all the time. And so I was able to buy Lilly for her birthday the earrings I had in mind. They are similar to those she was wearing when we first met and which were sadly lost in the fire in Héviz. Naturally they cannot compensate for the loss, for those earrings were an heirloom from her mother, but she was delighted by them. So you can see we are doing very well!

Send my greetings to Kurt and take care.
Yours affectionately,
Lajos

PS: The renovations ought to be finished by the end of the summer. Then you absolutely must pay us a visit.

19.

THE WRITER FEARS NOTHING SO MUCH AS HAPPINESS, WHICH is understandable, for writing is conserving, recording, ordering, but happiness avoids language, eludes words, hides in the past, and crumbles when you try to explain it. But as neither Lilly nor Lajos was a writer, they lived in their happiness like animals who waste no thoughts on the future and do not long for explanations.

They cherished most of all the hours before or after dinner with guests, when it was just the two of them. Getting ready together in the bathroom, dressing elegantly, putting on makeup and shaving, applying scent, exchanging glances in the mirror, and helping each other to fasten sleeves and necklaces. When they stood facing each other like that, they could not help laughing, for they knew that beneath all the jewellery and expensive clothes they were still the same children they had been when they first spoke to each other. Only, loneliness was no longer part of them.

After dinner and the ensuing conversations between the men in the smoking room and the ladies in the drawing room, the baron and baroness would often meet in the music room. Lajos loved watching her play, loved the way she closed her eyes and let her fingers glide across the keys, pressing the pedals with her feet, having slipped off her high-heeled shoes, losing herself utterly in the music. When she played, it was as if only her body was at the piano, whereas her spirit wandered through distant lands, shady forests and large cities, none of which Lajos knew, all of them foreign and unreachable.

When Lilly finished playing, she would sweep her hair behind her ears, stand up carefully as if she first had to get used to the gravity of this world again, and give a timid smile.

"Did you like that?" she would ask.

"Absolutely!"

"Really? Or are you just saying that because it's me?"

"It was heavenly, my love. I promise!" he would say, taking Lilly in his arms.

20.

But the writer also knows that happiness passes and they simply have to wait until it gives way to other feelings.

He had learned early on that as a man you kept your emotions to yourself or dealt with them with alcohol, and so Lajos hid his chin as deeply as possible in the upturned collar of his coat. All day long a herd of sheeplike clouds had been grazing over the city, and for reasons he could not pinpoint this made him feel melancholic. The stairwell smelled of wood, and the room he entered on the second floor of books, old rugs, and coffee. This took him by surprise, for he had been expecting the ethanol tang typical of doctors' practices. Lajos was reminded of the pain during and after his visit to the dentist the previous winter, and was happy that this treatment would not be as uncomfortable.

Mr. Király had narrow lips, pale-blue eyes behind thin lenses, and rosy skin, and Lajos sensed he was someone who preferred telling other people's stories to his own. But perhaps Lajos was just worried about revealing so much of himself to Mr. Király.

At any rate Lajos had imagined him very differently, as a serious, elderly man with a high forehead, white beard, and pocket watch, as a doppelgänger of Sigmund Freud, as he remarked. In fact, it turned out that Mr. Király had attended Freud's lectures on psychopathology at the University of Vienna, elated to be sitting in the same room as the father of psychoanalysis but failing to understand a single word. Nonetheless he had successfully completed his studies, returned to Pécs, and started his own practice modelled on that of his professor.

To begin with it was only wealthy women who came to see him, keen to talk to someone about their marital problems, depression, jealousy, or sexual frustration without having to listen to another's problems in return. But over time men too came to sink into the soft leather of the patient's chair.

Although he was not the first male patient, although people no longer entered the building as secretly and ashamedly as they would a brothel, and although his need to speak to someone was as great and urgent as his desire to sleep with Bertha, the German housemaid, he had never dared to arrange an appointment. But now he was sitting here, in this leather chair that was so soft it felt as if he might never be able to get up again, waiting for Mr. Király—who sat opposite, legs crossed, a notebook in his lap and a pen in his hand—to say something.

"Please begin by telling me what brings you here, Mr. Lázár."

Lajos blinked. He looked at the hands he had never needed to use for work. Looked at the signet ring with the coat of arms in the dark-green oval stone. It had been his father's ring. Ever since Sándor had drunk himself to death, Lajos had worn it on the little finger of his right hand, for it did not fit his ring finger. All the same, he could not banish the feeling that the ring was too big for him.

"I've thought long and hard about coming here, but always decided against it at the last minute."

He cleared his throat, unwilling to talk about the dream.

"What was it, then, that caused you to come in the end?" Mr. Király said in his velvet voice.

"A dream."

Mr. Király jotted something in his notebook; the expression on his face did not change.

"Can you remember it?"

Lajos hesitated, then nodded.

"Could you tell me about it?"

Lajos thought, thought about getting up and simply leaving. But then he did talk.

"I was standing at the edge of the forest with my back to our house. It was getting dark and I was peering into the forest, searching for something without being able to say what it was. The whole thing felt like a memory that did not belong to me. At some point I turned around because I was struck by the feeling that the house was no longer there. But it was. I went inside and everything was normal, only that no lights were on and lots of birds were flying through the rooms and corridors. The birds did not bother me, so I went into the drawing room to look at a photograph of my mother. She was young in the picture; it must have been from the time before I was born. When I picked it up to put it in my trousers—not in the pocket but in my crotch—the photograph disintegrated in my hand like porous clay. The paperweight with the red peacock shattered in my hands, and the empty yellow letters beneath it disintegrated too. Everything disintegrated the moment I touched it, even the birds who hung in the air as if turned to stone. I gathered them out of the air, every single one of them, and they all shattered in my hands."

Mr. Király nodded.

"Thank you. Now let us discuss the feelings that have brought you to me."

Lajos began with the safe things that did not frighten him and which he was able to speak about. He talked about the birth of his son, the sheer terror, the profound fear, and the incredible love he had felt when he held this being in his arms for the first time. How warm it was! And that heart, that tiny heart which beat and beat and beat! He spoke of what a struggle it was not knowing how to contend with the child. How he no longer knew how to live, that everything seemed contrived or wrong or too painful. As he spoke, looking all the time at the signet ring, he stumbled over memories of his father that had been laid open by the birth of his son.

"As a child I was convinced my father was a murderer. I don't know what made me think this; he was never violent, never hit or smacked us. When my mother was a child she was forced to kneel on dry maize kernels if she didn't finish what was on her plate—we never had anything like that. Although the idea was not anchored anywhere, I was certain he had killed someone. Sometimes I would even dream about it, always the same dream. Me lying on my side in bed in a red room, hearing my father creep up on me behind my back. I knew what he was planning, but wanted to spare him the embarrassment of being caught. So I pretended to be asleep and waited for him to thrust his long sabre into me and cut me in two. This is what I then felt, and at the same time I was watching it from above as if I were on the ceiling."

Here he paused briefly and looked into the corners of the room as if still more memories were lurking there. With his teeth he gnawed a cuticle from the bottom of a fingernail (a habit he had developed following the incident at the ruin and which he had been unable to break since). Then he continued talking.

"I never blamed my father for having killed someone, but only ever saw it as something that belonged to him, like his hooked nose or the scar on the back of his hand. After reading *Dracula* I believed that at night he turned into a panther who prowled through villages and forests. I was obsessed by the idea that during the day he did everything he could to protect us, suppressing his predatory instincts, and only came into my room at night."

In the days that followed this initial appointment, Lajos did indeed feel lighter. It was as if he had left his cares and memories there in the room. He also thought a lot about Mr. Király, who seemed to be someone who did not actually exist. This feeling persisted even after many sessions with him.

Two weeks later he was back in the brown chair, telling Mr. Király about his affair with Bertha. He could not (or did not want to?) remember how it started; all he recalled was that he was the first man she had seen naked. In all honesty it was a sight that had disappointed her. The aura of seriousness, wealth, and elegance that had surrounded him previously had gone. Instead there was an incredibly pale, uncertain man now standing before her, whose penis amused rather than excited her. Who had come up with that idea, that fleshy trunk dangling between the legs and that wrinkly reddish sack of skin behind it? Had the situation not been anything but funny, she would have burst out laughing.

But while she undressed, she watched as his excited heart industriously pumped blood into his penis, making it grow and grow. By the time she was wearing nothing but shoes and stockings, he had changed again. The ridiculousness had given way to something predatory, his expression dark and his breathing heavy. For a moment she considered running away, but that was not an option in her state of undress. So she stayed, also because the fear soon turned into curiosity and excitement.

Lajos said yes when asked if the infidelity weighed upon him.

"Can you tell me what induced you to embark on the affair?"

The baron looked past Mr. Király and tried to make out the titles on the spines of the books. He knew that Mr. Király had placed the shelves behind him to reinforce his professionalism, but it merely disconcerted Lajos. It gave him the feeling that he would not be able to get away with any lies.

"After the birth, my wife was naturally too exhausted to have intercourse, which I accepted, of course. But the child is now more than half a year old, and it does not look as if things will change in the near future. Along came Bertha . . . But that's not my issue."

"What is your issue, then, Mr. Lázár?"

Lajos looked at his fingernails and thought about this.

"I'm not sure. But without sexual intercourse I feel less masculine."

"Are you telling me that sexual intercourse is a sort of validation for you? A validation of your masculinity?"

"Yes, perhaps," Lajos said.

"Do you have any idea where this need for validation comes from?"

Lajos shook his head.

"Can you remember a situation in which you felt robbed of your masculinity?"

Lajos blinked and tore a cuticle from his left thumb. Ventured a glance into the pale-blue eyes. Weighed up his chances of getting a lie past the wall of books. Thought of his visit to the dentist, which had been far less painful. Remembered the long white candle in Melker's hand.

Then he divulged everything. It was the first time he had talked about it. He had always thought it would be easier to keep quiet. But this was not the case. By talking about it he brought it out of himself, brought it into the light where it became an object like the candle in the garden, only that the balance was restored rather than upset.

Mr. Király had put the pen away and now merely listened. When Lajos finished, he said, "Look, this isn't a part of you; it's something that happened to you. Something that you hid inside yourself out of shame until you believed it was your fault. But it's not. It was never your fault."

SHADOWS

21.

THE CHILD WHO HAD BEEN USED AS AN EXCUSE FOR EIGHT months now was called István. But that name was only heard when he was naughty. If he was quiet and good, they called him Pista.

For most of the time Pista lay in his cradle, motionless and silent like an object that only his beating heart and attentive eyes distinguished him from. If anyone bent over the crib, he would look at them inscrutably, like an animal. He never returned a smile or imitated a sound. But if he was given a rattle or something similar, he gripped it firmly and would not let it go.

Bertha, whose expression was not misted by maternal love, found the child sinister. The vehemence with which he clutched the toy without playing with it made her shudder. To her it seemed that the child was interested only in possessing these objects and preventing anyone else from enjoying them. She could not understand how the baron and baroness could call this emotionless creature Pista so lovingly, and whenever they stepped over to the crib or held the child in their arms she tried to see the shudder in their faces too. In vain.

For a long time the child did nothing but crawl. He crawled around the entire house, down the long corridors, up the broad staircases, into the kitchen and the blue room in the west wing, behind the curtains and under the beds. Lilly began sobbing several times daily because Pista was nowhere to be found, and Bertha would spend most of her time wandering after the child or crawling herself beneath tables, beds, sofas, and chests of drawers, looking for him.

Once the child even crawled into the fireplace, behind the logs, where he was found, black from coal and cold ashes, only when the elderly servant Béla, who could barely see anything anymore and was forever mislaying his spectacles, lit the tinder and heard the screams.

After the boy had finally learned to walk, it took another year for him to be able to speak, and this newly acquired skill allowed another oddity to seep into his behaviour a few years after that.

The baroness was sitting in the shade of the gazebo, putting the finishing touches to the seating plan for the banquet they were planning to give the following week. It was mid-July, the garden was blooming, the sun was high in the sky, and the air was thick with the scent of flowers, grasses, and fields. Wearing a light, bright-green silk dress, Lilly was just wondering whether to sit the young Hungarian writer visiting from Vienna next to Dr. Török or the director of the combustion engine factory when she heard Pista talking to someone. Shocked, she got to her feet and turned around—but nobody was there. Little Pista was standing alone by a young birch tree. He looked adorable in his dark-blue sailor suit, unbelievably so! When she saw him like this, from behind, she could not understand why she sometimes hated him so much, or was even afraid of him. But whom had he been speaking to? Here there was only the birch tree, the grass, the marble statue with the bare breasts, and the bushes at the end of the garden.

No sooner had she sat back down than Pista began speaking once more. She stood up again, and again he fell silent. Unsettled, she swept her hair behind her ears. Something was bothering her. But what? She screwed up her eyes and put up her hand to shade them. Scanned the garden. Looked out for something moving. But there was nothing. Everything was still, crushed by the heat, overwhelmed by the large sun, veiled by haze. The dry grasses, hard and yellow, thrust skyward; the light-green leaves of the birch hung statically in the air; the shrubs stood still; the statue remained petrified. But no, not everything was still. Pista's left hand was rotating continuously while his arm hung limply and the rest of his body was frozen. To Lilly he looked like a device in which a grain of sand had become caught in the mechanism, disrupting the whole thing.

"Who are you talking to, Pista?" she said.

He remained silent. He did not even turn, but just continued to move his hand in and out.

"Pista?" she said. "Pista, who were you just talking to?"

No reaction. She trembled at the thought of his face.

"I want you to answer me, István!"

Nothing.

"Answer me!"

The hand stopped turning. He spun around, smiled at her, and said, "To the shadow."

"The shadow?"

"Yes, the shadow of the birch tree. It's my friend."

"The birch tree is your friend?"

"No, not the birch tree. The tree is dead. Its shadow is my friend."

"Stop talking nonsense," the baroness said strictly.

"But it's true. Shadows talk to me. Your shadow does too."

Lilly felt herself becoming giddy and hot, her bones softening and her vision beginning to shimmer. Her silk dress stuck to her body, enveloping her like a second skin. Exhausted, she sank into the straw chair, clutched the armrests, closed her eyes, and heard Pista, in the distance, resume his conversation at a murmur.

Pista felt drawn not only to those shadows he spoke to as if they were people, and in which he moved as if sunlight were as damaging to him as it had been to his father when he was a child, but to every sort of darkness. He preferred dark clothing, was fascinated by the gloomy cellar vaults that seemed like the house's subconscious, and he longed for the short days of winter and twilight hours when the light retreated, the brightness decreased, and the shadows became longer and more numerous. On his sixteenth birthday he even dyed his hair dark with an infusion of sage, nettles, and rosemary.

Sometimes he would get up at night, creep into the drawing room, and spend hours gazing at a painting that mesmerised him. He had done this even as a small child, before he was able to speak, and he found it perfectly normal. The picture showed a deserted studio, in the middle of which stood a small table with an ashtray and glass of red wine. In the ashtray was a cigarette, smoke still rising from it. In the background, on the right of the painting, you could see an easel with a stretched canvas on which a blue undercoat had been painted. In front of the table, though not visible in the painting, lay the corpse of the painter—Pista could sense its presence.

The night seemed like an ocean from whose dark waters he had emerged. In the night he and his shadow were identical, and his inner self corresponded to the outside world—for everything was dark, the sky was black, and the garden lay there silent and deserted. And if your eyes had not yet become accustomed to the darkness, you could not distinguish between the garden and the night sky, so you might think the stars were flowers, shining brightly on tall, dark, black plants.

22.

One of Lajos's favourite sayings was "Speech is silver, but silence is golden." Indeed there were many things you kept tight-lipped about. Photographs of you with aristocratic friends from Germany who supported the fascists were torn from albums. Affairs hushed up. Knowledge of dirty dealings taken to the family grave. Relatives who had fallen in love with prostitutes or other men erased from the family tree. Childhood traumas suppressed.

What could not be said was written down and then safely preserved. That way you did not have to be constantly carrying secrets around.

The death of Lajos's parents was one such example. Pista was told that his grandmother had drowned. And his grandfather had simply fallen down the stairs. Tragic, it had been deeply, deeply tragic, but things like this happened.

What had been written in the family register read differently:

Mária von Lázár, née von Gampel, 16 May, 1870–8 April, 1913, suicide by drowning.

Sándor von Lázár, 28 November, 1868–6 June, 1919, skull fractured under the influence of alcohol.

The register went back to the eighteenth century. Numerous lives with all their successes and failures, entanglements and affairs, dreams and fears, illnesses and penchants, broken hearts and sleepless nights captured in a simple dash. And following the dash, the reason for the end of all of these things, recorded with nothing more than a short sequence of characters that made death appear as the only logical thing, and life as utterly fragile. An excerpt reads like a Gottfried Benn poem:

Peritonitis
Vomiting and diarrhoea
Suicide by gunshot
Heart attack
Puerperal fever
Suicide by hanging
Exhaustion
Typhus
Suicide by arsenic
Cerebral palsy
Anthrax
Suicide by falling

Another incident that was kept quiet occurred during the night of the banquet that Lilly had been planning in the gazebo, before she fell unconscious.

A few hours after dinner, which Pista had taken with Bertha at the small, round table, he woke up with the feeling of being befouled internally. For a while he lay perfectly still in an attempt to catch one of the dream images still flickering behind his hot brow. He thought that to rid himself of the feeling of rotting from the inside out, all he needed to do was to remember. But this would not work; images of his abdominal wall covered with a blackish-brown furry mould kept thrusting into his mind's eye.

Eventually he threw back the bedclothes from his feverish body and got up. It was pitch-black in the bedroom. As he paced up and down without turning on a light, he sensed the mould slowly being sluiced out of his body and being replaced by another feeling that made him toddle through the tall double doors, whose handle he just measured up to, and into the adjoining playroom.

Objects he had seen hundreds of times, tin soldiers he had led into countless battles, all of it seemed changed in the wan moonlight. He took this in without surprise; it seemed only natural that things should wear a different countenance at night. His gaze alighted on the fibres of the Turkish carpet. Unlike the other objects that he could have described flawlessly without omitting a scratch or worn part, he had no proper picture of this in his head. Until now its pattern had evaded him; all Pista had retained of the carpet was its deep, dark blue, across which he sent his toy ships to foreign, tropical shores where cannibalistic savages shot poisonous arrows at them from mangrove thickets. But now that the blue had lost its radiance in the semi-darkness, the patterning seemed to unfurl before him for the first time, gaining in depth and complexity from the moonlight and night-time shadows that slanted onto the carpet.

He stood before it, his bare feet on the cool parquet, feeling like one of those men he sent across the ocean; the ocean's surface was the carpet and below that it descended thousands of metres, ever farther until the powerful inky blue passed into a deep-sea black, calling for him via the face in the pattern, which existed only in the moonlight and was totally detached from the caramel-coloured hands that had once unconsciously woven it into the carpet. Time collapsed.

When he was finally able to disengage from the pattern, it felt as if a part of him were still down there. Without a thought he grabbed the craft scissors from the desk and, clasping them in his small fist, he left the playroom.

In the corridor he became aware of the silence that had surrounded him the whole time, but which had not had the space to spread out. He waded through it slowly, down the corridor, wondering what happened to it when you spoke. Then he was standing outside his parents' bedroom door. The feeling in his stomach became a pressure in his lungs; the sensitivity of his perceptions diminished. He was dulled, vacuous, and determined to enter the room.

The reading lamp with the China-red silk shade on his mother's bedside table bathed the room in a reddish glow. The light touched the bodies too, although it made them look smooth and bloody rather than velvety and soft. But this is not why Pista stops short in distress in the doorway. What causes him to freeze is the creature with four legs and four arms that his parents have combined to create. Although he can still make out his mother's upper body—which, braced on its bent arms, is being pushed deeper into the pillows with every thrust—from that of his father, the legs growing from the torrid centre of the panting creature are indistinguishable.

Are those still his parents? Their faces have distorted into hideous masks, their teeth are shining bloodily, the pearls around his mother's neck are glittering like pomegranate seeds, and the groaning and rumbling sounds coming from their throats seem to be bursting forth from their deepest, darkest cores. Moreover, the creature lacks all reason, any self-control, anything human. Stolid and destructive, mechanical and compulsive, it thrusts the sword into its own flesh. And Pista? He cannot tear his eyes away from the hellish scene being played out just a few steps from him and yet in a completely different world.

When the struggle finally came to an end, twitching and tremulous, moaning into the steamy air and screaming into the pillows, the creature fell apart. Lying on the bed again were Pista's parents, who only now became aware that he was standing in the doorway. They hurriedly pulled the covers over their naked bodies and told him to go back to bed. But he just kept standing there in silence. Now they noticed the scissors too.

"Why have you got those scissors?" Lajos asked.

Pista said nothing, his eyes dark and wide.

"Come on, I'll take you back to bed," Lilly said, having slipped on her nightdress under the covers.

No reaction.

"Come on, Pista, let's go back to sleep. You're so tired you can't speak."

She stroked his hair with her hand; he would never forget its smell of salty-sour sea, onions, and saliva. Meanwhile Lajos wondered how Lilly could change so quickly from her role as wife into that of mother. Even after six years he was still unable to find his way in his role as father. He had always believed it would simply come to him.

But this was not the case. Of course he loved his child, mostly at any rate, or at least from time to time, but often he would contemplate lifting the boy out of bed, holding his little nose and mouth shut, then laying him back amongst the pillows. Maybe that way it would be possible to return to their earlier life, in which hours like the one they had just enjoyed were not the exception and he did not need to pay a weekly visit to Mr. Király to be able to somehow keep living.

23.

In 1931, a year before Eva was born, Lajos came back from Budapest late one evening and saw, as he parked the car with a crunch on the gravel, that the light in their bedroom was off. At once he regretted not having spent another night in the capital. He could have gone to the casino or ordered a girl to his hotel, but now he had to lie in bed with his wife, who these days only slept with him when he forced himself on her. Her damp breath. Her warm body. The smell of sleep. The grinding of her teeth.

He decided to have a glass of whisky. He lit a cigar too, fully aware that these would not suffice, he would need the third anaesthetic as well. At least he was honest with himself. And knew that the feelings of guilt and resolve to finally be faithful again would be no match for his desire. Now that his mind was already on those white thighs, there was no point sitting here and tormenting himself any longer. He stubbed out his cigar and emptied the glass of whisky.

The baron entered without knocking and was delighted to find her in a nightdress. Bertha gave a start, her eyes wide and mouth open. And, as ever, it excited him to see her like that.

Once she had regained her composure she opened his trousers, took out his penis, kneeled in front of him, and closed her lips around it. He placed his hand on the back of her neck. And felt like a man once more.

All of a sudden his wife is in the room. A ghost with black eyes and light-blonde hair. White flowers embroidered on her nightdress. She stands there, watching.

He does nothing either, says nothing, just thinks about how he can get out of this trap he has set for himself. Out of this unfamiliar life he slid into when his own one slipped away from him. Before he can find an answer, Lilly turns around, glances briefly in the mirror hanging on the wall beside her, and leaves the room.

24.

They had started off driving with the roof open, and now it was closed, as Lilly wanted to sleep. In the morning, fog spirits had danced across the fields and meadows, but the higher the sun climbed, the more they retreated into the forests and riverbeds. Now the sky was cloudless and broad; the silver eagle on the radiator flashed in the sun.

Lajos loved driving the Adler Diplomat. The noise of the engine, the whirring of the tyres, the speed, the scent of the leather, and the idea that the vehicle was as powerful as sixty horses reassured and satisfied him. On a day like today he could not imagine anything more lovely than to drive through a green summer landscape with the window down, which is why he was also an advocate of the Reichsautobahn, the *will of a man turned concrete*, as he had read yesterday in the newspaper. Lajos did not know what to make of him—

On the one hand, of course he was ridiculous with his toothbrush moustache and his irascible gesturing, contemptuous with his brutality and hatred for the Jews.

On the other, Lajos admired his theatrical talent, his ability to play to the gallery more effectively than anyone, and his megalomania, which was so infectious that an entire people believed him.

Lajos had fallen for him too. It was not that he shared his political views—God forbid that he should go that far given his Jewish brother-in-law—but now and again, when things got too much or in moments of uncertainty, he would catch himself wondering what the Führer would do in this situation.

* * *

Lilly's head was resting on the window, her mouth slightly open. He looked at her and smiled. Since she'd caught him with Bertha, their relationship had improved. He had followed Mr. Király's advice and told her about his feelings. Then he had dismissed Bertha, replacing her with an elderly widow who had grown up in Germany and spoke excellent English after having spent many years as a secretary in Bombay.

In other respects too life had treated them kindly. Although the world economic crisis had not passed them by, thanks to their various sources of revenue it had hit them more gently than the majority. They bore up well, helped their peasants where they could, and continued to sell their meat, cereals, wood, and fish in the region. When prices gradually rose again, they had their meat and fish transported by train to the capital, as in the past, and sold in the market hall.

For the past year the combustion engine factory had been recording a profit again, allowing them to buy a four-storey house on the Danube. It was high time for such a move, as no matter how lovely the manor house was, the capital was where life happened. They now spent the winters there, attended balls and threw some of their own, went regularly to the opera and the theatre, took part in Sunday services, and at the picture house watched films in which people now spoke too. Their life was good.

"For now!" his sister would have called out, pointing a menacing finger. "Life is good for now, but only because we have money and happiness. Who knows for how long that will be the case?"

Since the Bleichröders had left Berlin three years earlier and moved to Vienna, Ilona had changed. She no longer listened to music, had taken up smoking, and barely left the apartment. Often she would lie in bed until lunchtime. She staunchly rejected a course of treatment by Freud, which Kurt had tried to persuade her to sign up for, saying, "It's not me who's ill, but the world." She saw future Nazis in everyone and was convinced that in Vienna they would soon be threatened by the same fate that had befallen them in Germany. Ever since the first statutory regulation of the Reich Citizenship Law the previous November, her husband had counted there as a *Mischling* of the first degree and she herself as a whore.

In view of this she was of course glad to have moved to Austria, but the fear of financial ruin and another war had pursued her. Anti-Semitism too was not a phenomenon restricted to Germans. Although neither Kurt nor she was of the Jewish faith, nobody cared about this given his surname was that of a rich, powerful Jewish banking family.

When Lajos stopped to fill up and stretch his legs, he recalled the summer of 1933, which Lilly, Pista, one-year-old Eva, and he had spent with the Bleichröders in the south of France. It was a beautiful summer, hot and dry. They whiled away their days by the sea, swimming and lying on red rocks. At night they listened to the gentle lapping of the waves through the open bedroom window, licking the dried salt from their skin. They ate mussels, lobster, and fish, and drowned their cares in white wine and laughter. At the time Ilona even believed that everything would turn out alright. After all, the Jewish boycott in April had been broken after only a day thanks to widespread passivity—surely that was grounds for hope.

That autumn, their skin still tanned from those weeks on the Côte d'Azur, the Bleichröders did nonetheless leave Berlin. Although the boycott had failed, it had led to a massive loss of customers and deposits at the banking house. The hatred towards Jews that had already been simmering below the surface during the lifetime of the powerful Gerson von Bleichröder had, since the National Socialist takeover, become the most important mark of a good German.

But Lajos and Lilly had not noticed any of this until now. They had not seen any of the anti-Semitic signs—JEWS NOT WELCOME—that Lajos's sister had talked about, and the only thing yesterday's edition of *Der Stürmer* had reported on was the Summer Olympics. All the same, he could not dispel the feeling that he was in some gigantic theatrical production.

This is probably why he was so angry that Ilona had talked of nothing but Hitler and his kingdom of shadows during their stop in Vienna en route. He realised he would not be able to shrug off her apocalyptic talk so easily. And yet it was such a wonderful day!

Morosely he got back into the car, handed the money for the petrol to the attendant through the window, plus a tip, then regretted it when in his rear-view mirror he saw the man stick out his right arm as a parting gesture.

It was only another half hour to their friends' villa. Lilly had woken up at the petrol station and was holding her hand out the window.

"As if the air were on fire."

Lajos did not respond.

"Don't be so worried," she said, putting a hand on his thigh. "An adjustment like that isn't easy, but your sister will pick up again soon. She simply needs to get used to her new life."

"I know. It's just strange that she's become so anxious. The only thing she used to be scared of was the forest. Nothing else. Now she sees ghosts everywhere."

"But that's understandable. Put yourself in her shoes."

"But you can't just stop living. She has children and a husband. She can't lie in bed until lunchtime."

"Lajos . . ."

"What?! It's true. She thinks the world revolves around her. And because she's not in a good way, she's leaving everyone else in the lurch."

Lilly took her hand from his thigh and looked at him.

"Don't compare her to your mother."

Lajos shrugged and put on his sunglasses.

* * *

Their friends did not like children and had none of their own, which is why Lilly and Lajos always visited them without theirs. They enjoyed this free time in which they could return slightly to being the children they had been when they had met in Héviz. The everyday responsibilities and cares fell from their shoulders. They sat on the terrace, drinking champagne, talking about the wealthy defendant the husband was representing, and gazing at the blooming garden, which the wife looked after. The neighbouring property belonged to Leni Riefenstahl, who was the other major topic of conversation.

"She's smart and terribly friendly!" they had said last time on the telephone. You forgot how famous she was and all the people she knew.

"Sadly we won't be able to introduce you to her. She is going to be frightfully busy because she's responsible for all the photography at the games. Apparently there's going to be a film too." Which was a good idea, they added. After all, the world had to find out what a great and progressive nation the new Germany was!

As they drove slowly past all the villas there was no sense of the coming spectacle. In this neighbourhood they seemed not to have a sense of anything. The lawns were freshly mown, the hedges neatly clipped, and the houses gleaming white. Here every day was a Sunday.

When Lajos turned the Adler into the driveway beside the unassuming two-storey Villa Riefenstahl, he spotted a roebuck at the edge of the patch of woodland that bordered their friends' garden. It was standing perfectly still, its head raised, its ears cocked vigilantly. Lajos could not help but think of the hunting season that would soon begin again, and the feeling that enveloped him when he shouldered his rifle at daybreak and went out to the men he set off with to shoot the animals in his forest. The shudder in those mornings, in the knowledge that they would be killing today. And afterwards, sitting at the edge of the forest around wooden tables covered with white tablecloths, drinking copious amounts of wine and eating bacon and goulash soup. And later in the afternoon, when the light was at its most beautiful, sticking a twig into the mouth of the slain deer and standing behind it in a semi-circle for the photograph, rifles hanging casually from their shoulders, then sitting in the smoking room beneath the English hunting scenes, which he loathed and yet hung throughout the manor house and everywhere in their city house too, simply because it was so normal.

Lajos shook his head, got out of the car, and shut the door. The roebuck disappeared into the wood.

25.

WHILE SHE STOOD NAKED BEFORE THE WOMAN WHO FELT HER body, Ilona thought of Zuckmayer, who had said, "The most important thing is our dignity. We must not allow ourselves to be stripped of that!"

But if you had to bend over stark naked in front of the wife of an SS officer, to allow her to inspect every part of your body thoroughly, this was easier said than done. Fortunately Ilona had not lost her ability to withdraw into herself like a tortoise, deep inside to a place where nothing could reach her, so that her body felt like a shell when the woman touched her between her legs.

At first she had not recognised Zuckmayer on the train, but his large, angular head and prominent nose had seemed familiar. And yet both she and Kurt had cried with laughter when they watched his play, *The Captain of Köpenick*!

The man had looked so serious as he sat there in the compartment that it would not have crossed her mind he might be somebody capable of writing such comedies.

When the train left Vienna's Westbahnhof at ten past eight, they did not exchange any words, but merely nodded to each other and then kept silent. Even the children were quiet, though they had been rendered speechless for days by their parents' tension, which was palpable in every movement.

Despite his pacifism, or perhaps because it was a world so alien to him, the military exerted a fascination on Kurt which could change to disgust in a matter of seconds, and it was only when he brought himself to ask the man about the medal on his lapel that the latter opened his mouth.

He did not want to speak about the war itself, but he did talk about being presented with the Iron Cross, 1st Class.

"The Kaiser looked as if he had rowed across the River Styx back into our world. His face was grey and as stiff as his short left arm, making it seem as if the moustache were sticking to a mask. But what I remember most clearly were his eyes. They were wide open, but they looked straight through me. As if he were already able to see his country's fate in the distance."

From the war the conversation had quickly shifted to the current state of the world, which was heading inevitably towards another war.

"My brother knows Ödön von Horváth," Ilona said. "If you read his new book you realise that there has to be a war. The young people haven't been prepared for anything else."

"Have you read the book?" Kurt asked.

"Yes, Ödön is a good friend of mine. I write too."

"No, really? What a coincidence! Might we know of any of your works?"

"You might have heard of *The Merry Vineyard*," Zuckmayer had replied modestly.

It was, of course, highly embarrassing that they had failed to recognise the writer, which is why they raved even more enthusiastically about his comedy afterwards.

They had seen the play before the Nazi takeover, or at least prior to the boycott that had induced them to leave Germany a few weeks after their holiday on the Côte d'Azur. And yet the boycott had been nothing in comparison to the past three days in Vienna, which Zuckmayer would later describe in his memoir: "That evening all hell broke loose. The underworld had opened its gates and let out its basest, vilest and foulest spirits. The city transformed into a nightmarish Hieronymus Bosch painting. Lemurs and demi-demons seemed to have crawled out of the filth and climbed out of boggy holes in the ground. The air was filled with an unrelenting screeching, shrill, wild and hysterical from the throats of men and women who kept the screaming up for days and nights. Everyone's face disappeared, replaced by grimaces, some contorted out of fear, others out of lies and others still out of hate-filled triumph."

Indeed they had not dared leave the apartment for fear of being beaten up, arrested, or—as they saw from their window—forced in front of a crowd of curious onlookers to scrub off the pavements the pro-Austrian slogans with which the supporters of Kurt Schuschnigg had tried to register their protest against the "Anschluss." But the fear was present at home too. Each time they heard footsteps in the stairwell, they were terrified somebody was coming to plunder their apartment.

Several hours into their journey Zuckmayer had asked—quietly, because the children had been lulled asleep by the monotonous rolling of the train's wheels—how much money they had on them. After exchanging a brief glance, Ilona and Kurt said, "Enough to get by for a while."

"That's too much," the writer replied. "You're not permitted more than twenty-five marks."

"We've hidden it, obviously," Kurt said.

"They'll find it. And then you might be on the next train to Dachau."

They exchanged glances once more, now disconcerted.

"First they'll search your luggage and the children's; then each of you will have to get undressed until you're completely naked."

She had glanced again at Kurt, but now he was looking pensively out of the window. Beside them the train's shadow glided across the green fields. Then they entered a short tunnel, in the darkness of which even the children looked like shadows. And that is what they were, in a manner of speaking: small shadows that followed them wherever they went, whether it be to Zurich, New York, or Dachau.

When the radiant early-spring light flooded the compartment again, Ilona said, "It's too big a risk, Kurt. We should be happy just to make it over the border."

Kurt nodded. They still had some money with a British bank that would suffice for their journey onwards and a modest new beginning, and with the rest of their fortune they would have to support the NSDAP, whether they liked it or not.

"I'll pop to the lavatory, then," Ilona said. "Will you see to the suitcases?"

Kurt nodded again. But was this the right decision? Should they really throw all their well-hidden money out of the window? Maybe the officers would not find it; perhaps they would not even look for it in the first place and just wave them through. How would Zuckmayer know what things were like at the border? If he had already been there, surely he would not be sitting here now, but somewhere by Lake Zurich or in a Parisian café.

Kurt got up, took the suitcases from the luggage rack, and opened them. From the corner of his eye he noticed Zuckmayer's hands. It was hard to believe that all they did was write. Those were a worker's hands, the fingers too fat for typewriter keys and too large for a pen.

I bet Ilona will like them, Kurt thought. As well as the medal on his lapel, as if he knew precisely how to score points with her.

But Ilona had not noticed the hands. She was standing in the cramped train lavatory wondering what to do with all the banknotes she had fished out of her bra, stockings, and panties. For a moment she considered merely flushing the money onto the tracks, but then she was not sure this really was the right solution. So she sat on the edge of the toilet and closed her eyes. The wheels of the train rattled through her head. She wanted to cry, but no longer knew how to. Had her mother been here, she could have done it; she would have cried until everything was better. Ilona missed her. Sometimes when she was certain that everyone was asleep, she spoke to her, asked her for advice even though she realised that her mother knew how to live least of all. And yet she hoped for an answer, any answer, just once.

When they stopped in Innsbruck at five o'clock and officers with swastika armbands boarded the train, she was pleased she had thrown the money out the window, despite the painful sight of the banknotes fluttering in the wind.

With a trembling hand she gave the man with the green, feline eyes their passports. Fortunately the name Bleichröder meant nothing to him. But when he read that Zuckmayer was a writer, he ordered him to leave the train there and then with his luggage.

The writer vanished into the station building, and the train continued onwards. It could happen that fast.

The female officer instructed her to get dressed again. She had seen what she wanted to see.

Ilona left the cell and stepped outside. The air was cold and clear, the sky glassy green and cloudless. The body and luggage searches had taken all night. Soon the sun would be coming up.

The children had indeed been made to take their clothes off too, even twelve-year-old Tony. As the mother, she had to wait by the door. Tony had wept and called for her, and for the first time in her life she felt that perhaps it was wrong to bring children into the world in the hope that things would be alright somehow.

Early in the morning the train left the border station of Feldkirch. When they crossed into Switzerland, the sun shimmered on the grainy corn snow.

26.

THE HOUSE WAS PART OF A TERRACE RIGHT ON THE DANUBE. Behind it lay a public park where, at the end of October when they moved to the city for the cold months of the year, the leaves on the trees were a golden yellow and the afternoon shadows long and talkative. Pista soon made friends with them, whereas in the monastery school over the other side of the river he kept to himself.

Before they bought the house in Budapest, he had been taught by private tutors, which meant he had barely any contact with people his own age. Although guests were forever paying visits to the manor house with their children, most of the time he hid from them in the cellar vaults or the forest. He was thus very unnatural in the way he behaved with his peers, something that immediately became apparent at school. He was an outsider, unfamiliar with the code of conduct, the way of speaking, the humour, and the class hierarchy; nor did he have the opportunity to learn these because once you were at the very margins it was impossible to make your way into the middle.

The only role that befitted him was that of scapegoat, whipping boy, and doormat. Whenever the solidarity of the class was threatened, he was held responsible for the tension, which he dispelled by being put up against the wall behind the school building. There they took turns in smacking his face with a ruler.

Pista soon discovered that any attempt to make himself invisible was pointless, so in the remote, barely conceivable hope of ultimately becoming stronger than his fellow pupils, he began twice daily—after getting up and before going to bed—doing press-ups until his arm muscles could take no more.

He liked the fact that this pain was his own achievement rather than anything to do with his tormentors. And while to begin with he only sensed that something was happening inside him, after half a year he saw the first changes. His upper arms were finally broader than his forearms and his chest no longer resembled that of a hunger artist.

To make swifter progress he now began to integrate weights into his training and whenever possible he would carry his little sister Eva around. Muscle ache became his constant companion, through which he developed a feeling for his body for the first time; previously he had regarded it as a vessel filled with, and controlled by, his thoughts and emotions. But now, through the aching muscles paralysed by exhaustion, his body came into its own. Pista became a being of substance, a body with weight.

Two years after the first press-ups, he was in fact stronger than the others. This even though he had always been convinced he would be weak, thin, and sickly all his life, as if his sensitive nature must be reflected in his outward appearance. Now his inner and outer beings stood in a contrast only he knew of. For the others, who could not see the uncertain, anxious child within, he was like a new person. He was no longer made to stand up against the wall, and even the teachers did not dare chastise him.

This was also due to his eyes that had lost their greenish-blue colour and instead assumed a hard grey hue. He had changed in other ways too: his face was more angular, the shadows beneath his cheekbones darker, his gait more upright, and his self-confidence greater.

Because of this transformation, which made him look older than the other boys, as well as his quiet, mysterious manner, he came to the attention of a girl at the school opposite, who, one Friday in November 1938, at the end of the day during that brief period when the girls and boys from the two schools came streaming into the small square between the buildings, brushing arms for a few thrilling minutes and their voices and scents mingling, handed him a love letter with a coy smile.

Pista read the letter on the way home, his heart beating wildly and his knees feeling weak. After having read it over and over again, he sat on the stone steps of a house and stared into the void.

When the church bells rang six o'clock and he realised he had been sitting there for an hour, he got up and hurried home, where he darted straight into his room so he could read the letter once more. But it had gone—

He looked for the letter everywhere, felt every pocket, turned out his satchel, and even slipped back out to trace his way back to the Chain Bridge. But he could not find it.

When, finally, he was sitting at the dining table, it struck him how dry his mouth was and how strange the taste inside it—

He was no longer able to discuss trivial matters at the table. All he wanted to talk about were the letter that somebody had written for him and the sweet phrases that this afternoon had still belonged to the girl with the brown hair, but which now were in his belly. He left the table pretending he had a bad stomach ache.

Although Pista could barely remember the girl's face the following morning, he spent the entire weekend polishing an equally passionate letter, which he handed her without a word, his cheeks flushed, on Monday in the after-school hustle and bustle. Then he sat in the park behind his house until it got dark. The sky was overcast and the world without a single shadow. A cold wind blew the brown dried leaves across the grass slope. So this was what it felt like to be in love—as if an autumnal storm were raging through your body.

A routine soon became established. They would pass each other letters in a two-day rhythm, without saying anything, for their voices were too shaky and their mouths too dry for spoken words. They would cast down their eyes and smile shyly. No sooner were they round the first corner than they would read the ardent letters that contained the entire contents of their little hearts.

Once he knew every word, Pista would scrunch up the letter and eat it. Then, with the bittersweet taste of the perfumed paper in his mouth, he pulled down his trousers and underpants, stood with his back to the bedroom door, closed his eyes to avoid having to see the two church towers with their black cupolas on the other side of the river, and chanted her declarations of love. When he sensed he was coming, he cupped his left hand and squirted his dark sperm into it.

As he had no idea what sperm was supposed to look like, this did not faze him. Only when it became lighter and more transparent each time he masturbated was he perturbed. It seemed unnatural that something from inside him should be so light. His concern became so great that he even stopped masturbating for a few weeks, though this ended when he came in his trousers in the middle of the square, having touched the back of Matilda's hand.

He was caught in Matilda's spell, caught in the web of words that she wove every evening in the light of her beeswax candle. Whatever he was doing and wherever he was, he saw her large brown eyes, her lips and hands, her brow, the collar of her blouse, the down on her cheeks, and the brooch on her chest.

Even in his dreams she appeared to him, always in uniform and accompanied by the red peacock that had freed itself from her chest, its tail with its black eyespots darkening the sky.

27.

At some point the letters were not enough. Matilda wanted to hear how her name sounded from Pista's mouth; Pista wanted to know how Matilda saw him. This is why, one clear winter's day, he put his hand in hers instead of a letter. Although surprised, she did not let go but pulled him along to the small park near her apartment. There, on a bench beneath a linden tree, she had read all of his letters.

Now they stood, still holding hands, in front of the bench, clueless as to what to do in such a situation.

At the entrance the park keeper was raking the gravel path, but otherwise it was empty.

"What now?" Matilda said.

This was the first time that Pista had heard her voice. He had imagined it differently, but that did not matter. She felt familiar at once.

"I don't know. But I'm liking holding your hand."

"I like it too."

"Let's not stop, then," Pista said.

Matilda nodded.

When night was falling and she had to go home, Pista stood and held out his arm as he had seen his father do and in films. Matilda laughed without his knowing why, but took his arm all the same. They left the park like this, nodding sheepishly to the keeper who closed the gate behind them, then walked in silence down the street, happy not to be alone when the gas lanterns lit up.

"This is the most beautiful moment of the day," Pista said, and Matilda said at the same time, "When the lamps come on, it always makes me feel wistful."

They looked at each other and laughed.

Outside the door to Matilda's building they faced the same problem as before: neither of them knew what to do now. How did you bid goodbye when you had sat holding hands and chatted together for an hour? Why were such things not learned at school? Why were you taught how to calculate the volume of the pyramids at Giza or the velocity of a falling leaf, but not how to live?

"What now?" Pista said.

"I don't know. But before you go could you say my name, just once?"

Pista felt himself getting warm. He peered over his shoulder, looked up and down the street as if about to do something forbidden. Then he said the name that in the past few weeks he had thought and written about more often than any other word in his life.

"Thank you," Matilda said. Standing on tiptoes, she pulled herself up by the collar of his coat, gave him a kiss—a real, proper kiss right on the mouth—and slipped inside before he could say anything.

28.

MATILDA SPENT THE REST OF THE EVENING IN THE BROOM cupboard. At eight o'clock she was allowed out briefly to go to the lavatory and fetch her blanket and pillow; then the door was locked again. The room was small. So small that Matilda, who only came up to Pista's shoulders, had to curl up to be able to lie down. The air inside was stuffy. All night Matilda's nostrils were filled with the smells of detergent, mouse poo, and old rags. But the worst was her mother's voice making its way in to her through the keyhole for hours.

Having locked her daughter in the broom cupboard, Mrs. Telkes had moved the rocking chair in front of the door and put on dark lipstick. When Matilda heard her voice, she flinched. There was scarcely anything she feared more than a sermon from her mother. Although nobody knew if she believed in God, she had studied the Torah in such detail that its strict rhetoric, steeped in allegory and symbolism, had penetrated her own language, in which she now conjured up images of coarse men's hands, broken flowers, nighttime parks and murky alleyways, shining black eyes, thighs with blood sticking to them, sabres that split you in two, extremities that grow inside you, arms and legs that fight their way out of the body, swollen bellies, agonising cramps, and the feeling of no longer being yourself. Even hours later, long after Mrs. Telkes had wiped off the lipstick with the back of her hand and lain down beside her husband, Matilda was unable to banish the images. The darkness had become saturated with them.

The following morning Matilda had to go to school as normal. But the world did not feel normal at all. Her mother's nightmarish images still stuck to her hair and skin; in her mind she kept reliving the hour with Pista, kept hearing her name from his lips until his way of saying it seemed to be the only right one.

Finally the bell rang!

Matilda leaped up and hurried out onto the square to meet Pista and tell him everything—

How, after their kiss yesterday, she had gone upstairs and been met by the question of where she had been all this time. How she ought to have recognised by the coldness in her mother's voice that this question was merely a test.

"I was in the park with Eszter," she had said, surprised at how unfamiliar she sounded. Maybe you're not the same person all your life, she had thought. Maybe you're a variety of people who think, feel, and look differently, and are only held together by the same name.

"I see. You were with Eszter in the park. That's alright; she seems to be a good girl," her mother had said.

"Yes, she is," she replied, not hearing the clattering of the ice cubes in her mother's throat.

"Then I'm sure she cherishes her mother, instead of talking to her with a serpent's tongue that makes lies sound like truths."

It was then that Matilda understood. Of course, her mother had seen her from the window. Had seen them wander down the street arm in arm, had seen her standing down there by the door, had seen his lips form to speak her name and her lips kiss his. She should have known. How careless she had been! And how incredibly stupid then to lie to her mother!

Now she had to be more circumspect, especially over the next few weeks. She and Pista could exchange only a few words at most. She had to return home punctually. Had to record her feelings in letters again and hope that her mother would soon forget the matter.

She had to destroy Pista's letters that she stored in a box under the bed. It would be best if she ate them, for in the dustbin her mother would find them; smuggling the fat bundle past her and getting rid of it outside would be too risky, and she could not burn them in her room either.

Outside the school gate stood Dora, the Telkes family's housekeeper. When Matilda saw her waiting there with her broad, hanging shoulders and a basket full of market vegetables in her arms, she stopped at once. In vain; Dora had already seen her and there was no other way out.

"Come, my child. Let's go home," she said. Her eyes were full of such sympathy that Matilda was moved to tears. Dora laid a heavy arm around her shoulder and said, "Even though it doesn't seem like it at the moment, it will get better. You know the saying: Time passes and waits for nobody. Not even pain."

"But why is Mother doing this to me?"

"Because she loves you, my child."

"She doesn't love me; she hates me!"

"No, she doesn't. If she hated you she wouldn't be so worried about you."

Matilda wiped her face dry with the sleeve of her dark-blue uniform.

"So what should I do now?"

"The best thing would be to forget the boy. And if you can't do that, there will be a way," Dora said, hoping and praying that she was right.

29.

After not having seen her for a whole week, he was handed a letter by her friend Eszter. Unable to wait until he had left the square, he read it there and then, amidst the throng of pupils emptying out of school.

Afterwards he staggered like a drunk through the streets, across the bridge, and into the park behind the house, where he unsuccessfully looked for a shadow that might comfort him. The shadows knew a lot but were not well versed in heartache. And so he went home, even though he had wanted to delay this for as long as possible. Avoiding his mother, who was learning Italian in the study, he crept up the four storeys and past his sister's bedroom, shut his door silently behind him, went over to the window, and gazed at the Danube, its grey-green waters drifting past so slowly that he could scarcely make out its flow. Nevertheless, the driftwood and all the other flotsam would eventually reach the Black Sea, the gathering place for times gone by, broken dreams, and lost things. But Pista was not thinking about this. He was not even thinking about Matilda anymore, as he had done uninterruptedly over the past week, only about how he could escape this feeling of being mauled, this feeling of being torn apart by an entire pack of bloodthirsty hounds. Jumping out of the window would be one possibility. He would be dead instantaneously, no question; after all, falling down the stairs had been enough to finish off his grandfather.

But he knew he would not do this, that he was merely playing out scenarios in his mind as a distraction. For there was still a chance of seeing Matilda again—at some point. And a world in which this opportunity existed was a good world.

* * *

Weeks passed in which they did not catch sight of each other. By the time the monastery school bell rang, four minutes after that of the girls' school, Matilda was already three streets away. She was still being escorted home by Dora, who felt sorry for the girl and could not understand Mrs. Telkes. What was so bad about meeting a boy? Particularly as he had accompanied her home. What did it matter that he was not Jewish? After all, the Telkeses were not proper Jews themselves anymore. And perhaps it would be no bad thing to marry a non-Jewish boy, considering the developments in Germany. Who could predict what was going to happen? Maybe Hungary would be threatened with the same fate as Austria.

Matilda was not interested in any of this. Although she heard her parents talking about it, she could not hear the anxiety in their voices, the fear their words were dipped in. Besides, it had nothing to do with her, this country everybody was afraid of. Why should she be interested in politics when she could neither sleep nor eat for heartache?

By now even Mrs. Telkes was worried, and she instructed Dora to cook only Matilda's favourite dishes, as she believed her going hungry was a form of strike intended to blackmail her. But Matilda really could not manage a mouthful. Everything repulsed her, tasting like warm sawdust, even Dora's pancakes with apricot jam.

On the occasions that she did eat something—if only three fried potatoes—it would lie heavily and undigested in her stomach, causing her to toss and turn for hours in bed.

Pista's suffering was no less painful—

For a long time he used to go to bed early. Sometimes when he had turned out the light, his eyes would close so quickly that he did not even have the time to say: I'm going to sleep. But now that sleep was his only hope and release, he seemed to have lost the ability to nod off.

He would lie awake for hours, staring into the darkness that had settled in his room, and allow his thoughts to revolve around Matilda. If he switched on the bedside light and checked the time, it was always midnight. The hour when an invalid, who has been obliged to start on a journey and to sleep in a strange hotel, awakens in a moment of illness and sees with glad relief a streak of daylight showing under his bedroom door. What luck, it is morning! The servants will be about in a minute; he can ring, and someone will come to look after him. The thought of being made comfortable gives him strength to endure his pain. He is certain he heard footsteps; they come nearer, and then die away. And the ray of light beneath his door is extinguished. It is midnight; someone has turned out the light in the corridor, the last servant has gone to bed—and now he must suffer all night long.

And so it was. He suffered until it was morning, and then he continued to suffer until it got dark again. But worst of all were the brief phases of sleep when the red peacock fanned its tail, from which the image of Matilda then emerged. She surfaced from the lust for which he had no outlet, but from the margins of his dreams he imagined that she was the one giving rise to this desire. He could feel her warmth passing over his body, and he pressed himself to her—only to wake up at that very moment. Then his unhappiness was greater than ever, and he resolved the very next day to muster his courage and simply walk after her. Or go straight to her parents and ask for her hand in marriage.

He had to do something, for the letters on their own were inadequate. How could he express his love in them? Everything he wrote sounded banal, kitsch, or foolish.

Matilda saw it differently. For her there was nothing lovelier than his letters. All the same, she tried every day to persuade Dora to allow her at least a glimpse of Pista, for what she feared more than the Old Testament tongue of her mother was forgetting his face. She could already sense it slipping away from her.

At the beginning of her quarantine she had seen this face constantly and in razor-sharp focus (even though the two of them had hardly dared look at each other on the bench beneath the linden tree), but later she had to strain, even at night, to recall the colour of his eyes or the shape of his nose.

"I know the curves of his handwriting better than that of his lips, Dora. I have no idea what he smells like, and soon I will have forgotten what he looks like. Then I'll be loving him and writing to him every evening without a face in front of me. Surely you cannot want that!"

No, she did not, but nonetheless she pulled the unhappy child closer to her and said nothing.

"I ask almost nothing of you! All I want is to stand in the same square as him and look at him. Just for a minute, that would be enough! I don't even have to speak to him. We could simply wait and watch him come out of school."

So it went on every day, all the way to school and back. Only when they were in the stairwell did Matilda say nothing, for she was still hoping that her mother would soon forget the matter. It was her only chance of hearing Pista say her name again, for she could not expect any help from her father. Mr. Telkes had contradicted his wife on only one occasion: fifteen years earlier when he had said he was not ready to become a father.

"Yes, you are," Mrs. Telkes had said, and when he shook his head, she had walked off in her fur coat—and nothing else—and rung the doorbell of his best friend.

At the end of March, Eszter handed Matilda a letter that Pista had rewritten fifteen times to make it sound as optimistic as possible. After having discarded the fifteenth attempt too, he fished the first one out of the wastepaper basket, smoothed it out, and put it in an envelope. The time of confidence was past.

When Matilda read the letter on the way home—for Dora allowed her to do this at least—she began to cry so bitterly that the housekeeper grasped her shoulder more firmly than ever, terrified the girl might throw herself in front of the next car.

Matilda did not stop crying until she was at the front door to their building. "You've got to calm down now, my child," Dora said. "The whole of Pest will soon be underwater otherwise!"

But of course she understood Matilda, for she had not forgotten the summers of her own childhood, the endless hot summers that had unfolded before her like a fan of shimmering yellow days. She could, therefore, imagine how dreadful for Matilda the thought must be that she would not see Pista again until the autumn. At the same time she knew that although the first few weeks were bad, the memory of them, like everything else, would fade under the summer sun. Despite this, or perhaps because of it, she decided to grant Matilda her wish. They would see each other one last time before he went to spend Easter in Héviz, and from there continue on to the manor house.

The time came four days before Pista's departure. During the previous week a cold front had drifted over the country from the north-east, bringing snow and frost again. The farmers had cursed and prayed, the park keeper had wept over his flowers and cherry trees, and Matilda had written Pista's name on the fogged-up windowpanes.

Now she was standing at the edge of the square beside Dora, whose hands were in her coat pockets because of the cold, feeling more nervous than the day when she had put the first letter into the hand of the silent, strong boy who always stood in the shade.

When the bell of the monastery school rang, the square was deserted, for the sun had already disappeared behind the building, and it seemed as if the cobbles, now in the shade, had not been warmed for centuries. Beneath the windows of the school lay dirty heaps of snow, shovelled from the square, on which yellow light from the classrooms fell. Having already flowered, the trees had been taken by surprise by the sudden return of winter and now were at a loss as to how to keep growing.

"Is that him?" Dora whispered excitedly as the first boy left the building.

Matilda shook her head.

"What about him?"

"No."

"That one?"

"Not him either."

"The one behind?"

"I'll tell you when he comes."

But when he did come, she said nothing. Dora nonetheless realised that it must be him. Matilda froze, muscles tensed, eyes open wide in terror, like a deer at the side of the road that remains paralysed long after the vehicle has passed.

The boy had something of the deer about him too, the way he stepped onto the square and looked in all directions, as if he could sense their eyes on him.

When he spotted them, he moved his lips without their being able to hear what he was saying, then swept back the hair falling to the side of his brow before approaching them slowly and uncertainly. Matilda, who only now noticed that Dora's heavy arm, which she had become so accustomed to, was not around her shoulder, went up to him.

All of a sudden they were face-to-face again. Without letters they could have handed each other. Instead, Dora's eyes in her back, which saw them speak to each other, shift from one foot to the other to combat the cold, and then embrace briefly but firmly.

VOICES

30.

Whereas from the years before the war there are three photograph albums showing Lilly as a bride, Lajos as a hunter, the children in the swimming pool, the whole family beside the Acropolis or at the Bleichröders' in Berlin, from the war itself only two small, grainy photographs exist, both of Lajos in uniform—

In the first he is smiling beside his shining Adler Diplomat. The second shows him looking serious alongside other soldiers who, judging by their uniforms, were under his command.

Another pointer is provided by various articles about the life of a Benedictine monk in which the baron's name keeps cropping up. This baron who, on the morning of 3 September, entered his office, switched on the wireless, called for old Béla, who could no longer hear anything, then sat down when the servant did not come and felt increasingly weak as he listened. He then went straight back to their bedroom, knocked on the door to the bathroom in which Lilly was rubbing cream into her thighs, and said, without waiting for an answer, "Britain has declared war on Germany!"

Lilly opened the door and looked at him with an expression he could not read.

"It's war! Chamberlain has declared war on Hitler. He really had no choice after the Germans marched into Poland," he said again, even though he knew she had understood.

"What does that mean?" she asked, to prevent him from saying the same thing for the third time.

"That France will soon follow Britain's example."

Lilly continued to look at him like a child unable to grasp all of this. It reminded him of the day at boarding school when Caspar had told him that war was at the gates of Europe. At the time Europe had merely been an abstract concept for him, but that had not stopped the war from descending upon it. And now they were back in the same situation.

"I never thought there could be another war."

Lilly nodded and suddenly realised she was naked. She could not be naked at a moment like this! Britain had declared war on Germany and she had nothing on! War had returned to Europe and she was standing around totally exposed!

As she hurried past Lajos she glanced out of the window.

The apple trees bore a particularly large number of pears this year. The dress she took from the chair was hanging in the wardrobe. Lajos was an anxious boy, and time had been turned back twenty-seven years.

The outbreak of the war had barely troubled Pista at first. He could not imagine anything by it, for nobody spoke about the last war—the wounds that the Treaty of Trianon had left were too fresh and deep—and although Poland was not far away, it was not that close either.

When his father, who from the first days of the German invasion had done nothing else but read the newspaper and listen to the wireless, had still not returned to work by the end of the month, he began to worry. This stagnant existence was most unlike his father, who, with his agricultural talents, skill with money, and tireless hard work, had restored the Lázár name to its former splendour.

But his mother was behaving oddly too. For inexplicable reasons Lilly was relating everything to the war, which she had chosen to be the focal point of her world ever since the Red Army's invasion of eastern Poland, if not before. If, for example, he and Eva were arguing over the last piece of Dobosh, she would say, "Europe's at war and you two are arguing over a piece of cake. You ought to be ashamed of yourselves!"

When it rained, she said, "At least the weather is showing consideration for the global situation!"

Although the signs had been there, Pista was too preoccupied with his thoughts of Matilda to foresee the collapse of his world.

To avoid forgetting all the details and facets that Matilda consisted of, he had decided to think of her each time the bell chimed. Not that he would have failed to do this incessantly anyway, but his love was too great to leave it to chance.

For the very same reason, all summer long he had gone to bed as soon as the first bats appeared in the sky, to give him sufficient time as he lay in his room, the window open, listening to the chirring of the crickets and his parents' voices in the garden, to imagine Matilda in such fine detail that around midnight he believed she really was standing there beside him in her dark-blue uniform, with the peacock brooch on her chest and a letter in her hand.

No letter from Matilda arrived. Instead, at the beginning of October, one sat on Lajos's desk, summoning him to report without delay to the barracks in Pécs.

The following morning he got into the Adler, drove to Pécs, and reported for duty.

They were due to move back to Budapest in two weeks. But when Lajos drove home in the Adler that evening, he shattered Pista's happiness with just a few words. They would not be going back to the house in Budapest, but to one in Pécs that was only a few minutes' walk from the barracks.

"We're going to stay here for a little longer," the baron had said after returning from Pécs. "They want me to discharge my position as officer and help with the emergency preparations. We now share a border with Russia, and this is something that has to be taken seriously."

But Pista was not interested in the border. Let the Russians annex them and integrate them into their enormous barbarian empire that, like a ravenous monster, gobbled up everything it got its paws on, be it the Ukraine in the west, Kazakhstan in the south, Siberia in the east, or Finland in the north, which its insatiable eyes, as black as a black bear's, were already ogling greedily, and towards which it was already, almost imperceptibly, shifting its border, a border so long that only a mother like the Soviet Union could bring forth enough men to secure it. Let them come, the unwashed masses from the east, let them come, overrun them, and bury the whole of the west beneath them. If that meant he could see Matilda once more.

31.

EDMUND PONTILLER, THE UNYIELDING BENEDICTINE, ARrived several months later, in the spring of 1940. The baroness had already moved back into the manor house with the children while the baron had remained in Pécs and would only drive out to the country at weekends. He was the first person in many years to dare enter the forest without a rifle. Since little Ilona had been found unconscious there, people from the surrounding area avoided it. They told each other horror stories, talked about a strange town in the heart of the forest, and kept claiming to have seen the Thorn King or one of his seductive daughters at the forest's edge. When children were badly behaved, they were threatened with being abandoned amongst the trees.

Of course people warned the new chaplain, and he listened to all their superstitious gibberish, only to head into the forest a couple of days later with nothing but a notebook, three pencils, a water bottle, and the Bible. He was not afraid, for he knew God was on his side. What he also knew was that superstition could be fought only with deeds, not words.

That day he got up early, washed his hollow-cheeked face that, even with his fifty years, sported only a youthful fluff above the top lip, got dressed, sat on the edge of the bed, prayed with closed eyes, clasped hands, and bowed head, tied the laces of his hiking boots, shouldered the leather rucksack that he had packed the night before, and went down to the kitchen to drink a black coffee and inform the cook that he would not be there for lunch. Then he crossed the orchard and entered the forest that began just beyond.

* * *

Pista could not stand Pontiller for three reasons.

First, it was because of him he had to sit in sheer boredom on the hard wooden benches of their chapel on Sundays and Wednesdays (for these were "dark times").

Second, the chaplain was so terribly in love with life that Pista felt like taking his own. Even now that German troops had invaded neutral Belgium, he talked about how grateful he was to the Lord for the return of the spring, the resurrection of life, the carpets of snowdrops, daisies, and primroses, the rays of sun on the rear of the stable that helped the hawthorn unfurl its silky petals and stick out its bundles of gleaming stamens.

To Pista it seemed as if the Benedictine was less concerned with his faith and more with the beauty of nature, which, now that Matilda was at an unattainable distance, he himself could no longer take pleasure in. The glorious May days seemed phony, the blooming meadows gaudy, and the twittering of the birds a provocation.

"If Pontiller had been born three hundred years before our time, Humboldt would've had nothing left to discover," said the baron. "Our chaplain would have set out for foreign, tropical shores, converted cannibalistic savages in mangrove swamps, and returned home a great explorer."

Pontiller did not even regard the Bible as the greatest work of literature, but rather Proust's *In Search of Lost Time*, something he admitted only in a whisper and with a hand in front of his mouth; merely the frequency with which he talked about it made this clear. Indeed he spoke so often about Marcel—he always used the writer's first name—that one might think he were a close friend or even a lover. At any rate he considered Marcel to be a kindred spirit who would have understood him better than anyone else. And so it seemed as if his greatest regret was that he had never met the novelist personally, for he was certain that a conversation between the two of them would have been far more animated than the now well-known one between Marcel and Mr. Joyce, whom Pontiller considered an uncouth vagabond and with whom he was not on friendly terms, nor did he wish to be. By the time the two writers met in 1922 in Paris's swanky Hotel Majestic after the premiere of Igor Stravinsky's ballet *Renard*, Pontiller had already settled within the thick walls of a Lower Bavarian monastery to embark on his ascetic life, which in many respects resembled Marcel's in his Parisian soundproof cork-lined bedroom, though far removed from any high society.

Third, and finally, everyone else loved Pontiller. Although his father might make fun of him occasionally, saying things like, "I think our chaplain has forgotten that Jesus is the son of God, not his beloved Marcel," Pista knew that he liked and admired him. The baron was fascinated by the cleric's self-assurance, his trust in the world and God, and his ability to focus completely on the moment and on life. Lajos was unable to do this himself; he might exist in this world, but he was not part of it. It was always the world *and* him, and the world always seemed to be something threatening him, something he had to be wary of.

Lilly enjoyed Pontiller's presence too, for she missed the social life and intellectual buzz of the capital. This is why she would urge the chaplain every day to keep her company when she took her afternoon tea. If he did join her, over the steaming porcelain cups a fast-paced battle of words would ensue, in which Lilly kept trying to get Pontiller to talk about the war, while he invariably endeavoured to steer the conversation towards Marcel.

What disappointed Pista most of all, however, was that even little Eva, who otherwise adopted all his opinions unconditionally, liked the priest. She called him Edmund, and because of his child-friendly manner (he crouched down when talking to her) and gifts (from his extended walks he always brought back a flower, stone, leaf, or snail shell for her collection that was going to contain every object under the sun), he had her wrapped around his little finger.

He had just as easy a time charming the servants and the farmers from the surrounding villages. His gifts to them were his subtle friendliness, the calm in his voice, and the simplicity with which he expressed himself. He would never use a word unless he was certain that the person he was talking to would understand it. Inclusiveness was the basic principle to which he subjected his life. He only permitted himself to use highfalutin words and elaborate syntax in the imaginary conversations he had with Marcel, who was the real reason for his long walks, and in his letters to the archbishop.

Although Edmund Pontiller was an open person who laughed a lot and regarded the Church's earnestness as old-fashioned, Pista could not shake off the feeling that beneath this outward impression lay another truth that, similar to aquatic plants beneath the slimy-brown surface of a sleeping pond, where dragonflies and other insects whirr through the summer calm, was barely visible. This was down to the dark shadows in the corners of his eyes and the rings beneath them; on the chaplain's smooth youthful face they stood in such contrast to his sunny disposition that Pista could not help but interpret this darkness as the real representation of his character. Yes, he was sure that Pontiller was hiding something and determined to uncover what this was.

At some point the mask would slip, Pista knew, for the strain of keeping it up must be enormous. He just had to be there when it happened. To avoid missing this moment when the actor leaves the spotlight, quickly wipes the sweat from his brow in the darkness of the stage, allows his gaze to wander across the auditorium where the applause has subsided and the audience members are getting to their feet, then steps off the stage to remove his makeup in front of the mirror and become himself once more, Pista began to follow

Pontiller wherever he went and to watch him continually. Soon he knew every one of the priest's facial expressions and all the gestures with which he emphasised his own words or those of God; he could predict how he would react to certain questions, remarks, or sayings, and could perfectly imitate his gait as well as his manner of speaking. But still he did not know the face behind the mask.

At this time—a rainy May was coming to an end—Pista's nightmares returned. As with a cold, he had realised they had gone only when they came back. Here they were again, having been absent for . . . for how long and since when, in fact? Since Matilda. Ever since Matilda had handed him that first letter more than a year ago, his nightmares had been something from the time before her. Now, as they settled again over the dark plain of his sleep, colourless and flickering, overexposed and grainy, it was even worse, for it felt as if the time with Matilda was over, as if it had been a mere phase that now belonged to the past.

They were the same dreams. The same sequence of images that lined up haltingly, allowing them to be perceived as a single recording. And, as in the past, they gave Pista the feeling that he had no control over his life. Whereas during the daytime, even though he was not able to do or eschew what he wanted, he could at least maintain the illusion of enjoying free will over his thoughts, the moment he tumbled into the realm of dreams he had to relinquish even this freedom, the last one remaining. Sleep was like a rapist for whom he had to lie in bed every evening anew.

As in the past, the images showed Charlie Chaplin undressing as he danced, tossing the bowler hat from his head, throwing away his stick, removing the too-small jacket from his body, slipping off the too-large shoes, climbing out of the too-wide trousers, tearing the toothbrush moustache from his upper lip, and rubbing the make-up off his face, so that at the end of this disquieting sequence he stood there, a good-looking man, whose face nonetheless continued to look unreal, as if beneath the mask of the tramp he wore another, and another still beneath that one, as if he consisted of nothing but masks and had long forgotten who he really was.

July was unbearably hot and felt to Pista like an endless recurrence of the same day. He slept and dreamed of Chaplin, woke drenched in sweat, washed his face, washed his hands, and washed his pubic area, as if this might rid him of the dogged, pitch-black dream images. Then he stuck to Pontiller's heels, following him wherever he went. All day long he saw the priest's slim, black figure ahead of him, which under the blazing sun looked like a dream image itself, in the air that shimmered above the dusty country roads, hills, and fields, in loamy farms, gardens, and dried riverbeds, distorting everything.

At midday, when the sun cast no shadows, they would eat pepper salad or cold peach soup behind closed curtains. Then they would retire to the drawing room, also darkened, and long for the winter landscapes, frozen lakes, snowy riverbanks, and blizzardy roads that hung on the walls in gilded frames.

The sun burned mercilessly from the ossified sky, causing birds to fall dead from the trees. They hit the ground with a thud, forcing the gardener into the heat to gather them up before they turned soft. For late in the afternoon, when you thought the blood in your veins might be about to boil, individual heavy dark-grey drops of rain fell onto the blistering earth and steamed before you could take a look. But soon the isolated clunks would swell into a drumming that became more regular and sonorous by the second until the air was turned into a space you could reach into through the open window and where the thunder was barely audible, drowned out by the pounding rain.

Then all the curtains in the house would be pushed aside and the windows wrenched open, the roar deafening everything. The baron and the chaplain used this time to stage their verbal showdown, which Pista would listen to as best he could. He would sit on the gold-and-red-striped sofa, trying not to let his gaze that was fixed on Pontiller be lured outside by the quivering leaves and whooshing lilac bushes in the driving rain.

The downfall stopped as abruptly as it had begun. All of a sudden the flood dried up and a faded, tattered disc pushed its way through the blanket of cloud. Or a clear, golden evening sun tore open the dark storm clouds and sent its light in long, heavenly rays, reminiscent of those in altar paintings, down to the postdiluvian earth. At any rate the water evaporated within minutes, leaving the tropical humidity as the only reminder of the storm.

Pontiller would spend the rest of the time until dinner studying ecclesiastical writings, enjoying Marcel's prose that glittered with divine brilliance, or taking short strolls around the garden accompanied by Imre.

His conversations with Imre were even stranger than those he had with the baroness. For unlike everyone else, he did not speak to Imre as he would to a child or a dog, but treated him like an adult. Whereas Lilly and Lajos allowed Imre to sit at the table, but never asked him a question, never allowed him to speak at all, in fact, for fear that he might start talking about the forest, the hunter, or *Night Pieces*, Pontiller did not shy away from listening to everything that he had to say.

After dinner, the priest placed his right hand on his heart, made a slight bow, and withdrew from Pista's scrutinising gaze by leaving the table and retiring to his room. This was on the second floor of the western wing, ruling out any possibility of looking in from outside. To do this Pista would have to climb one of the trees on the edge of the forest, which at night was out of the question; he too knew the stories they told in the village.

He had no other option than to sneak into the western wing undetected and hang around outside Pontiller's bedroom. He spent hours like this, his ear pressed to the door, his lips chewed bloody with nerves.

On one of the last days of the month he heard footsteps at the end of the corridor—

They were the shuffling steps of old Béla, who no longer had the energy to defy gravity and lift his feet from the floor. The servant was even older than Imre; nobody knew exactly how old. Lajos believed the old man had died without their having noticed, but was unable to part from his profession and so he simply continued as a ghost. Lilly thought that was nonsense, but she was not a Lázár by blood and thus had no idea how obdurately the ghosts stood their ground in this family. Even Hayo Lázár, the solitary ancestor with his sixteen children, would sometimes call on the baron to give him a piece of well-meaning but antiquated advice.

As old Béla could scarcely see anything these days, Pista had enough time to hide in the neighbouring empty guest room. It was strange to see the room like this: isolated, dusty, and dark. He did not dare put on a light. Not because he thought that Béla might notice, but because he did not wish to disturb the room's atmosphere. It seemed as if it had a personality, which every object develops if you ignore it for long enough and it can break away from its human-related function. This is why he did not put on a light, and this is why he did not sit on the soft bed either, but on the hard chair by the wall.

Béla shuffled slowly past; then it went quiet. Almost, at least—

A voice, barely audible, travelled through the wall that the chair was against and which separated this room from the chaplain's. It was a man's voice that Pista had never heard before.

Pressing his ear to the wall, he held his breath. Who could this be?

The man must be standing close to the wall; now Pista could hear the voice quite clearly and yet he did not understand what the man was saying. It was German, but an odd, coarse, scratchy German that sounded as if the man had a problem with his vocal cords.

If Pontiller said anything at all, Pista did not understand that either. He listened and listened, for there was no end to the torrent of words—

Until he fell silent as if at the flick of a switch.

Again Pista held his breath expectantly, waiting for the stranger to leave the room. But it remained silent. No footsteps in the corridor. No sound from the room.

Eventually Pista left the dark guest room and went to bed, feeling as if he had just woken from a dream.

32.

In retrospect it seemed to Lajos as if he had done nothing during the war but read. This was not true, of course; he had, after all, been the officer of a motorised platoon. Not to forget that thing with the Jews. But the baron had indeed read a lot.

Unlike the chaplain, Lajos no longer read novels, poetry, or philosophical treatises, only the newspaper. He had developed an almost physical aversion to all fictional or beautiful prose, based on the view that it was wrong to write about anything but the war and even worse to distract from it with made-up characters, plots, and lives, with well-constructed sentences and theoretical scenarios. You had to face up to the truth, endure reality. Otherwise you ran the risk of ending up like Sándor von Lázár.

Lajos remembered only too well how, on the morning he found his father lying in his own vomit on an oriental carpet, carefully handwoven over the course of several months, he swore he would never become like that.

Nor had he forgotten that day when his father had ordered him to remove his shoes and walk barefoot through the hard snow around the house. "To finally freeze out the weakling in you," he had said, locking the door behind his son.

And yet his father had been no less weak himself, even though he had allowed his son to be treated only with the utmost severity and had never once held Lajos in his arms. This weakness was also the root of his lifelong fear of ending up like his brother Imre, from whose existence he was separated only by his strict daily routine. Had he not forced this upon himself he would have found it just as impossible to attend to business as well as administering the family fortune and estates. If this tightly laced corset of routine had not kept him together, his mind would have gone to the dogs too.

In Lajos, however, who exhibited the weakness Sándor so despised in himself in even greater measure, he was unable to tolerate it. He intended to drive it out of his son by an early toughening process, which succeeded only when, after everything had fallen apart following Mária's death, he gave up and showed his son what happened when you could not stomach the truth. When you had to drink to avoid thinking about what a weak person you were to try to shift the blame for your wife's suicide onto your children, to forget that you were completely alone and the world was now a very different one.

The time for poetry was over—

When Lajos returned to their house in Pécs on the evening of 20 November, 1940, he found a dark-blue collection of poems on his desk. Someone must have left it there, one of the servants, perhaps, or Lilly.

Lajos was exhausted. Hungary was now officially fighting on Germany's side. Today Miklós Horthy had put his signature to the Tripartite Pact. Lajos was not sure what to make of this. On the one hand, it was, of course, good to be on the side of the victors. But his erstwhile secret admiration for Hitler had turned into a deep contempt and dark fear. Late in the evening, like now, he could admit it to himself: he was afraid of Hitler as he had been afraid of his father.

To understand him a little better, to discover between the lines some clue as to the future course of the war and its next victim, he spent every spare minute reading the newspaper. If he came across one of the maps of Europe that showed the front line and every day larger areas marked with swastikas, his vision began to flicker a garish yellow and white as if the world were dissolving in acid before his eyes. Or he would feel so nauseous that he thought he was going to throw up. Nevertheless, the truth had to be faced.

Although the baron was so tired that he would have been happy to fall down dead, he picked up the volume of poetry. As he did so, it felt for some inexplicable reason as if the book had appeared on the table only when he set eyes on it. He sat in the leather armchair by the window and was briefly reminded of Mr. Király. Would it still have come to war if Hitler had undergone a course of therapy in that soft leather chair?

He switched on the small lamp on the dark walnut table and opened the book without paying attention to the title or author's name.

Along the blooming meadow's verge
We wander in the dense shade of trees.
Like a giant on the horizon, it seems,
As softly comes a summer breeze,
Stands the church spire, sunk in evening dreams.

Shadowless, up in the sky
The white ships glide on air.
The bells of the sheep intone
And at once I know where
All the years have flown—

As he lowered the book, Lajos noticed at once that he was weeping. He had not cried for years, which is why he now got such a shock. For a brief moment he worried he would not be able to stop the tears, that he would simply go on crying forever, but fortunately they soon dried up. These were probably the last he had left, he thought, for as a child he had cried so much that his reservoir must be drained.

He closed the volume of poetry and placed it on the coffee table. The feeling that had come over him whilst reading was the same as that which had accompanied him for years after the death of his mother. It was the feeling that the entire world known to him was a sunken city whose monuments and buildings, church towers and palaces were still just visible beneath the surface of the water, but whose time would never return.

33.

On 27 June, 1941, the Soviet Union declared war on Hungary even though Hitler had not planned for the country to participate in Operation Barbarossa, concerned that the Hungarian units were inferior to the Soviet ones. As proved to be the case.

Despite this, Joseph Goebbels noted approvingly in his diary in May 1942, shortly before another two hundred and fifty thousand Soviet soldiers were taken as prisoners of war at the Battle of Kharkov: "When the Hungarians report that they have 'pacified' a village, there is usually nothing left of that village or of its inhabitants."

Lajos stayed in Pécs, looking after organisational matters.

When ten-year-old Eva asked him why they were fighting against the Russians, he said, "To stop them taking the manor house away from us." But he did not know for certain; at the beginning of the offensive the Soviet troops had not been at all combat-ready.

Edmund Pontiller read the seven volumes of his beloved Marcel over and over again to avoid losing faith in the world.

The Hungarian soldiers and occupation troops looted, killed, and raped. Though the civilian population began by hailing them as liberators from Soviet domination, it soon wished the latter back.

Pista regarded the Russians as barbarians who ate with their hands, wore beards crawling with bugs, and had sex with bears.

Hungary hoped for a restoration of the status quo prior to the tragedy of Trianon.

Lajos looked after organisational matters.

Pista, who realised to his horror that he thought about Matilda only every few hours, tried to remember her again with every bell chime.

Sometimes he would creep into the still-empty guest room to listen to the mysterious voice. He lacked the courage to knock at Pontiller's door or enter his room.

Admiral Horthy, who, in the hope of recovering the lost territories with German help, had been moving closer to the Third Reich for several years, even introducing similar anti-Semitic legislation after the proclamation of the Nuremberg Race Laws, now sought a way of exiting the war without losing those territories conquered with German help, seeing as enthusiasm for the campaign against the Soviet Union had waned along with the prospect of an early victory.

After the Battle of Stalingrad, two hundred thousand Hungarian soldiers were encircled, at which point the government tried to establish contact with the Allies.

In the autumn, the Lázárs' car was confiscated. Before it was taken away, Lajos photographed the Adler Diplomat from all sides in the gravel driveway of the manor house—and remembered that seven years earlier, at the Olympic Stadium in Berlin, he had stuck out his right arm in salute as euphorically as everyone else.

During Advent, Pista wrote a poem about each part of Matilda's body. His greatest fear was to forget what she looked like. His second greatest: to never be able to sleep with her.

In March 1944, German divisions invaded Hungary from all sides. A collaborationist government was installed that soon afterwards began deporting the Jewish population.

Lajos looked after organisational matters.

The Jews had to be listed, labelled, stripped of their rights, expropriated, and ghettoised.

34.

IT LOOKED AS IF A FUNERAL PROCESSION WERE MAKING ITS way through the city. The faces were serious and anxious; some were crying, but subdued, as if they wished to avoid drawing to themselves the attention that should, after all, be on the dead. In the morning it had rained, but now the sun was shining. The road was gleaming and it was very quiet. As if the rain had washed all sounds from the world. Even the footsteps of the mourners, which appeared hesitant, were almost impossible to hear. This though there were many of them, three thousand five hundred people to be precise.

Although it was the beginning of July, they wore thick woollen or fur coats, which made for a bizarre image, as the onlookers standing in small clusters on the pavement were in summer clothes.

They stood together, hands behind their backs or resting on handlebars, watching without saying anything, without expressing their condolences. They whispered to one another, as if now that things had come this far it was impossible to talk about it in public. It also seemed as if there were an invisible boundary between the mourners and those by the roadside, as if the kerb were an insurmountable barrier observed not only by the onlookers, but also by the mourners, who hardly raised their eyes.

What would now be the point of looking at the linden trees lining the street, the shop windows, the old entrance to the house where the name by the bell had been changed, or the faces of old work colleagues, neighbours, and friends? Why bother looking at all of this in the hope of finding something to hold on to, seeing as they knew that everything had to be left behind and soon all that would remain would be the back of the person in front and their own toecaps?

At the front was a middle-aged man wearing an elegant hat and a brown jacket, and carrying a small cardboard suitcase. Over his other arm was a heavy coat. The yellow star must be on that, because there wasn't one on his jacket.

Lajos gave the man a piercing gaze in the hope that he would look up and see in his eyes that he was not like the others, that he did not despise them and had never wanted any of this.

But the man walked past him with his eyes on the ground.

Was he different from the others? His actions had been the same; what counted apart from these? What help was it to these people, who were participating in their own funeral procession, that deep down he rejected the regime he served? How did it change their situation that he wished Obersturmbannführer Eichmann and Ferenc Szálasi dead? They still had to proceed towards their demise. As had already happened so often. They were familiar with this, the funeral processions through the streets of their cities, across the fields of their country that had the highest population density of fascist, semi-fascist, and extreme right-wing movements. They were used to the looks of their fellow citizens, standing and staring from the pavement or from windows, as if they were an oriental caravan with decorated camels, exotic spices, and baskets of snakes.

The image was not new to Lajos either, for in April he had been responsible for organising their ghettoisation. All the same, he could barely look at them today. Back then they had been ordered to go into the theatre, so they could be counted and registered. The stars, printed on large yellow rolls of material sent from Berlin, were also handed out there. Then they had been taken to the workers' quarter on the outskirts of the city. Their apartments and furniture had been auctioned. This area, with streets stinking of urine and sick plane trees, had been fenced off on either side.

Now it was different. Awaiting them today was not the ghetto, where typhus had broken out due to the cramped living conditions and poor hygiene, but where they were at least all together—as Lajos had persuaded himself. Today it was one of the three goods trains that since mid-May had been transporting four thousand of them daily to Auschwitz.

Lajos stood in the shade of a linden tree and lit a cigarette. He had been chain-smoking since the German occupation. It helped against the tension, the fear. He was permanently terrified that someone would betray Pontiller and that one day the Gestapo would be at his door. At the same time he was nagged by the question of whether he was doing the right thing. For of course it was courageous of them to hide the priest who was being persecuted for his trenchant criticism of Hitler and the Nazi regime, but the fear of drawing attention to themselves and putting him in danger prevented them from helping the Jews.

He shook his head and stubbed out the cigarette with the sole of his shoe. No, that was not right. It was not that he did not want to put the chaplain's life in danger. It was because he was a coward. Since his boarding-school days he had looked at the ground to avoid standing out. To be spared. He had pushed and kicked others to avoid lying in the dirt himself.

He had looked at the ground for as long as it had been possible. Now he had to raise his eyes and look at every face—

These were all people with their own eyes that had seen things alien to his, with their own hands that had reached for other shoulders at night, with their own thoughts that he knew or had never thought himself, with their own lives that, despite everything, essentially resembled his. And yet only his had ever counted.

Towards the end of the funeral procession, his gaze fell on a woman who looked like Ilona. He quickly turned away, lit another cigarette, and stared at the milky-white sky. But it was too late; the thought was there. Of his sister running for the train with Kurt and the children. His sister who had escaped before it had come to this. Who now lived in the United States because she had never felt safe in Switzerland either. That country which had pressed Germany to introduce the red "J" stamp in the passports of Jews so that Swiss border guards and immigration officers could easily identify them, turn them away, and send them to a certain death, to prevent the "Jewification" of their beautiful country, which passed on the lion's share of the costs for its twenty thousand Jewish refugees to the Swiss Jewish community, itself numbering only eighteen thousand members. Although his sister and her family had escaped, in his mind he nonetheless saw them climb stiff-limbed from the train by the gates of Auschwitz.

35.

Late evening. After a hot, cloudy day that had ended with a downpour, the baron was sitting in his study with the window open, smoking. On the desk in front of him was a sheet of writing paper and a fountain pen. His intention was to write about the past few months and the thoughts that were torturing him.

The deportation was now two weeks in the past. The train from Pécs had been one of the last to reach Auschwitz before Horthy stopped the transports. Since the ghetto had lain deserted on the edge of the city, Lajos had been smoking more and more. Even while eating, which he had almost given up altogether, he always had a cigarette in his hand now. He had hoped that his consumption would fall again after the deportation, when everything was a little calmer and his organisational task complete.

The feelings of guilt had intensified too, for now that the Jews had gone, he could no longer comfort himself with the idea that tomorrow he might muster the courage to help them. Nor could he persuade himself that everything would be alright, for now they were dead and this was something he had to live with.

He was about to start writing when he heard a car arrive. The crunch of tyres on the gravel driveway, doors slamming, brisk footsteps.

Stubbing out his cigarette, Lajos got up, smoothed his combed-back hair in the reflective window, and left the room without bothering to glance at the vehicle.

He knew who it was.

The young servant with the crippled arm, whom they had

engaged to take on Béla's work without dismissing the elderly retainer, was already coming up the stairs to find him.

"The Gestapo!" the servant said, out of breath and in some agitation.

"I know," the baron said, wandering past him.

The servant followed Lajos and asked, "Should I say that you are not at home, Baron, sir?"

Lajos shook his head.

"No, there's no point in that."

"Should I warn the chaplain?"

"Tell him to come downstairs. And not to attempt any escape. That would be futile."

One of the police officers was blond with a pointy chin and ears that stuck out. The other's face was pudgy, red, and German through and through. Both were wearing spectacles, which confused Lajos, as if glasses excluded brutality and sadism.

Just as puzzling was the strident voice of the pudgy officer, which stood out in such contrast to his appearance that Lajos first fixed his gaze on the lanky one.

"As I'm sure you are aware, there is an urgent arrest warrant out for Mr. Josef Edmund Pontiller. It would spare us quite a bit of trouble if you could take us straight to Mr. Pontiller."

"I have already sent the servant to fetch him," Lajos said.

"That is most obliging of you, but we would like to see his room," the pudgy one said.

"Of course, gentlemen, of course!"

As Lajos went ahead, he wondered what would happen if one of the two officers were to shoot him in the back. Would he die instantly? Unlikely. If he were lucky, he would topple backwards and break his neck. Although it was more probable that he would fall forwards. Perhaps they would shoot him in the back of the head to save ammunition and to avoid having to hear his screams. In that case he *and* his father would have died of a fractured skull. Both on this same staircase, its steps covered with such a soft carpet that it was almost impossible to hear whether they were actually following him.

When they turned into the western wing, by contrast, their footsteps echoed so loudly that it sounded as if an entire troop were approaching. The baron tried to envisage how he would find Pontiller and the servant. He fleetingly pictured the chaplain lying in the garden with a shattered skull, having leaped from the window. Egon Friedell had taken his life in this very way. That was right at the beginning, when Austria had just been joined to the German Reich. When she threw herself at Germany. And yet the two SA men who had asked the housekeeper where Friedell was had not come to arrest him.

The chaplain had decided against death. When they entered the room, he was sitting on the edge of the bed, staring at the wall. At his feet lay a packed cardboard suitcase. When Lajos saw it, he was reminded again of the man without the star, whom he had been unable to get out of his head since the deportation. While he had harboured sympathy for the other mourners, the feelings he had for this man were quite different. For Lajos it was as if the man were hardly a human being at all, but much more a symbol that, though it existed in this world, was also removed from it and thus unassailable.

The chaplain gave the same impression. To the officers as well, it seemed, for whereas a couple of minutes ago their determination to come down harshly on him had been palpable, now that they were standing before him and he, contrary to expectation, had neither attempted to escape nor to put up resistance, this determination was merely a mask they wore, a posture they had to force themselves to assume.

"Good evening," Pontiller said.

In his voice was a calmness that reminded the baron of Chamberlain's address five years earlier, when he had announced to the

British people that they had declared war on Germany. It was hard to imagine that this man sitting on the edge of the bed, as if waiting for a taxi, and who had given the Gestapo officers a friendly greeting, could criticise the Führer in his sermons with an almost eerie eloquence and fury.

Although he had become more moderate since moving into the manor house, chiefly to avoid imperilling the Lázár family, when visitors had come and in other personal conversations, he had made no secret of what he thought about the dictator who was dragging Europe headlong into the abyss. He had not held back in his letters to the archbishop either, writing things such as: "There are still Catholics, and even Catholic priests, who praise to the skies this Nero on the German throne, defending him and trying to make his persecution of Christians appear harmless." It was just a matter of time, therefore, before somebody betrayed him to the local Gestapo, or the latter got hold of one of these letters.

While the chaplain continued to sit on the bed, staring impassively at the wall, the pudgy officer locked the door and asked the baron where the servant had gone, and what Lilly and the children were doing. The lanky one went over to the small chest of drawers beside the window and inspected the wireless.

"Very nice," he said. "Do you listen to the wireless much?"

"Yes, very often," Pontiller replied with a smile.

The lanky officer nodded.

He was just about to switch it on when it looked as if he had spotted something vanishing into the trees. For a moment he peered out into the darkness of the forest, which was deeper than that of the sky, then turned back to the wireless. When he fiddled with one of the black knobs, a strangely rasping voice rang out.

"What's that?"

Pontiller looked at him seriously.

"A Swiss broadcaster. If you keep turning you'll find a British one too."

"That's quite enough!" the pudgy officer bellowed.

Nodding, the chaplain reached for the suitcase and stood up.

"That's staying here!"

"But my Bible—"

"Leave it here, I said!"

Pontiller put the case down on the floor and was taken away. The baron, who walked behind them, thought of the costume balls that Lilly loved to organise. Two police officers and a Benedictine priest in a black cassock—

At the door Pontiller said, "Please give my regards to the baroness and the children. Thank you for everything and God bless you!"

Then they shoved him down the stone steps and into the black car.

36.

Lajos had recognised the sense of unease from the ghetto they had wandered through when he made his rounds. His uniform had been sufficient to numb the Jews with fear and dread. There had been no pogroms in the Pécs ghetto, as there had in Budapest and other cities, but here too the soldiers had behaved aggressively. In mid-June one had beaten an elderly man to death with the butt of his rifle, supposedly because of a disapproving look. The soldier had pocketed the glass eye that had popped out of its socket, as a souvenir.

Now that the ghetto was empty, its residents dead, and the Russian monster so close that it disintegrated into hundreds of thousands of battle-weary, dirty, sick, and hungry soldiers, the unease shifted to the groups of aristocrats. All day long they would telephone counts and barons who were their friends, send each other cards showing the actual position of the front line, only unsettling themselves even more with such a to-do. They told each other the terrible stories they had heard and which they did not dare reveal to their wives and children. They started reading the Bible again after many years.

To the outside world, Lajos presented a confident and strong personality; inwardly, the sense that he had never found an answer to life, not even to how to cope with it, exasperated him. Since Pista's birth he felt as if everything had slipped away from him for good, as if he could no longer act, only react. The time was past when, with his business nous, he had restored the House of Lázár to its former glory. He had merely spent the last few years not losing the family's wealth again. But even this had become increasingly difficult; events were developing so fast and so unpredictably that the baron was no longer able to keep up with them. He was as tired and battle-weary as the Russian soldiers. Lajos was forty-four and he felt like an old man.

When the Soviet troops were just a few days' march from Pécs, the Lázárs too decided to flee westwards. On the morning of 8 December they loaded two horse carts. On these were:

eight woollen blankets and counterpanes
three mattresses
two sacks of potatoes
three sacks of turnips
six suitcases of clothes and toiletries
three dachshunds
twelve sacks of horse feed

As they carried their personal belongings out of the house, wondering what else was important, Pista became aware of how many things he was surrounded by without ever having taken notice of them—

The stag's head with the fourteen tines above the fireplace. The gold-and-red-striped sofa in the drawing room. The bedside lamp with the China-red shade. The carpets in the corridors and on the stairs that swallowed the sound of footsteps.

All of these things comprised the space in which he had grown up, in which he dreamed, laughed, thought, and cried. Even if he were to start a new life somewhere far away, with a new desk and new lamp, these would only ever be copies of the original objects that appeared in his mind the moment he heard the words "desk" or "lamp."

They buried the jewellery and silver beneath an elderflower bush on the edge of the forest, threw the rifles into the water tank, and left the furniture in the house, in the hope that they might be able to return soon. The doors were left open so that the Russians would not smash the windows.

At eight o'clock they set off. It was such a cold morning that it was difficult to breathe. Although it was no longer snowing, the road and fields were white. Pista sat, a counterpane around his shoulders, amongst the potato sacks in the rear cart. He was already freezing even though they had been on the road for only a quarter of an hour. Beside him sat Eva, her eyes red. She was wearing an ermine coat of her mother's that was far too big for her, but much warmer than her own. On her hands were thick gloves.

She had been crying all night. Pista had heard her through the walls of the playroom that stood between them. But he hadn't gone to comfort her, to tell her that everything would be fine, and to lie beside her until she had calmed down. That was not the sort of thing that was done in this family

Sometimes it felt to Pista that you had to be ashamed of everything that was not visible on the outside: fears, digestion, thoughts, genitalia, and emotions. You even had to be ashamed of love—especially as a man. He could not just go to his father and give him a kiss, let alone ask him for one.

"Do you know how often my father held me in his arms?—Never! Not once!" Lajos had said, before shooing his son away.

Not only did they hide their love from each other; they did not articulate it either. Pista could not recall ever having told his parents that he loved them and admired them despite everything. Whenever such words lay on the tip of his tongue, something held him back, as if it were a confession and he a defendant in court.

He had no idea where this feeling came from, but he knew that his parents felt the same. They hardly ever showed him their love either, causing him sometimes to wonder whether it existed at all.

Perhaps they did not love him at all and the only thing that had prevented them from abandoning him in the forest when he was a child was social convention.

Even from his mother he had received barely more than a fleeting peck on the brow, and whenever he was lonely or frightened, it was Bertha, not she, who had come to sit on his bed. But her words had never been so comforting, her kisses never so lovely, as his mother's, for he knew that she was being paid to look after him.

It is almost impossible to imagine you will have to flee the following morning. Pista had not been able to do this either, and even in retrospect their flight seemed inconceivable. All that remained was the feeling—

The feeling of leaving everything behind.

The feeling of travelling westwards, without knowing where.

The feeling of his teeth chattering so badly from the cold that he thought they were going to fall out of his mouth.

Scarcely any images remained in his head—

The road, full of people, carts, donkeys, and horses.

Old Imre, humming away to himself.

The perambulator with squeaky wheels.

The two invalids, bent crookedly on crutches, crawling across a field to shorten their journey.

The simple houses they passed and which made him think that he might have gone to comfort Eva had they lived in one of those with fewer walls.

Eva's body hurt. She had not known that the cold could be so painful. Now they had been en route for several hours. To begin with she had cried, but she stopped once they reached the big road. She was too old to cry in front of other people. Besides, the trek was moving so quietly, as if it were made up of mute people. All she heard was the icy wind carrying the barking of dogs across the fields and getting caught in the few bare trees by the side of the road, the snorting of the horses, and the squeaking of the perambulator.

It was being pushed by a young woman with a large jute sack on her back. She was alone, talking to nobody, looking at nobody either, just continuing straight ahead.

Eva was fascinated by the woman and had not been able to take her eyes off her since they had first started travelling alongside her. She was not beautiful—her nose was too big, her skin pallid, and her hair looked like black wire—but she had an aura that captivated Eva.

When she tried imagining where the woman came from, the first thing that came to mind was the seventeenth century, which she knew from the paintings of Vermeer, whom Edmund (thanks to Marcel) revered. The chaplain had shown her his book of reproductions so often that the women depicted in them seemed more familiar than the servants in the manor house. Eva could not get enough of these women, all of whom had stories of their own that Vermeer merely hinted at, lives into which he never offered more than the briefest glimpse, as if he considered it important to leave them with their secrets rather than reveal them. It was self-evident to the artist that the love letters being read while standing at the window, or the thoughts being pondered while putting on a pearl necklace or pouring milk into a bowl, were no-one else's business. Perhaps this was also why he had not written, and kept as far away as possible from writers who, in their compulsion to formulate the whole life and every thought of their characters, no matter how personal, raped and pillaged people's private lives. He did not understand how they could be so inconsiderate as to write their characters into a fictional reality, there to dissect them before everyone's eyes. For this reason he only recorded moments, positioning his characters almost always by windows to give them the opportunity to look out from this frozen world of colour and oil.

Eva was also especially fond of Vermeer because unlike most painters he never depicted women without clothes. Paintings of naked women triggered in her an unease she had no words for yet. Whenever she looked at a picture like that, Eva always thought of the same two things: her own body, which she compared to those of these women painted by men; and the fact that the woman who had modelled for the painting had had to undress in front of the clothed painter and stand there like that.

The woman with the perambulator reminded Eva of Vermeer's women. She could not say for certain why, but it had something to do with the unconditional way she pushed the perambulator ahead of her, similar to how the maid poured the milk into the bowl or the woman read the letter by the window. Just as those characters existed for their actions and the moment captured in the painting, she seemed to live for the pushing of the perambulator and walking along this chaotic road.

Eva's parents, by contrast, appeared as forlorn and intimidated as the peasants who had come to the manor house to ask the baron for school money for their son or a small contribution to the cost of their daughter's wedding, and were taken by Béla through the entrance hall and up the carpeted staircase to the study with the massive mahogany desk, tall window, and paintings of the house on the walls.

Her mother was sitting on the same cart as them, while her father was on the other beside Imre, who hummed constantly and regarded the whole thing as one big adventure. The baron was wearing a thick coat and felt hat, but otherwise looked indistinguishable from the peasants in their flat caps. This was also what made him sit there slumped, his dulled eyes gliding impassively over the blinding white landscape and long procession of freezing people. For ever since the self-doubt, which had temporarily left him during the period of his business and social successes, had returned, and he no longer felt able to cope with the responsibility, duties, and tasks of a baron, he was dependent on this external superiority that reminded him he was still a baron, even if he no longer felt like one. But now that he was fleeing westwards like all the others, with nothing except horse feed, a suitcase full of clothes, and a few provisions, there was no longer anyone to acknowledge this superiority with lowered gaze and hands nervously kneading their cap. Yet now he needed this acknowledgement more than anything to prevent himself succumbing to fatigue.

He did not know when this feeling of exhaustion had come over him, in the same way that you cannot remember the appearance of the first, barely noticeable symptoms of an illness. The decline crept up on him, imperceptibly, disguised as the simple weariness that sometimes manifests itself when you contemplate the life still ahead of you, with all the decisions that will need to be taken and all the mistakes that will be made in the process. But soon all his thoughts were under control. The baron was like a madman who realises his mind is slipping away but can do nothing about it. He sensed himself falling to pieces inside and checked his most routine actions for signs of neglect.

If, for example, he realised that he had uttered a word with insufficient clarity because his tongue was too lethargic, the next time he took particular care to articulate this word cleanly, only to stumble over another. If he was lost in thought, he often forgot things, such as replacing the cap on the fountain pen. The more he resisted his decline, the faster it appeared to proceed. For this reason the ignorance of others was the only thing still keeping him together. While this continued, his decline remained something that could be hidden and hushed up.

It was a puzzle to Eva how the young woman, who was wearing nothing apart from a thin coat, headscarf, and black skirt, could keep going. They had seen some people standing at the side of the road, breathing heavily and totally enfeebled by the cold. These were mainly elderly people whom the others had passed by in silence, unwilling to add yet another burden to the many they already had.

The sky was so white that it was almost impossible to differentiate it from the snowy landscape, interrupted only by the two black lines behind the two invalids crawling across the field. And circling in the sky were individual ravens that looked like shadows and reminded Eva of Béla's face. Since his vision had almost gone and he had begun to hamper daily life at the house rather than facilitate it, he had been regularly telling a story designed to teach morals and human compassion.

It was about a blind man whose parents had died and who was thus taken in by one of his sisters. But as he was unable to help out on the farm he was treated like a beggar. They invited the local peasants over and for their amusement gave him wood, leaves, and mud to eat. When that became boring, they started hitting him in the face, laughing at his twitching eyelids and pitiful efforts to defend himself against the blows. Moreover, he had to go out begging, even in winter when there was thick snow and it was deathly cold.

On one such day the ground was so frozen that a burial in the village had to be postponed. In the morning, his brother-in-law had taken him to a main road. He left him standing there all day long, and when night came, he told his people that he had been unable to find him again.

The blind man stood by the road for hours and waited. When evening came and he felt he might freeze to death, he simply walked off. Several times he fell into a snowy ditch; he sprained his ankle in the furrows and kept getting to his feet in search of a house. Eventually, when the hour was late and his weak legs could no longer carry him, he sat down and never got up again.

His corpse was not found until springtime when the snow melted and a large flock of ravens kept circling above the plain, descended like a black rain cloud, flew off again, and kept returning.

Whenever Béla told this story Eva felt ashamed at being human. She would wish she was a dog, a spider, a stool, a tree, even a raven—just no longer a human being.

Béla had wrapped three blankets around his shoulders, for in the confusion he had mistakenly put on his light rain jacket. Although he never stopped telling the story of the blind man for fear of being abandoned himself, he would not have admitted to the difficulties he had coping with everyday life, or sought help.

Eva would have loved to ask the woman with the perambulator whether she would like one of their blankets, but she did not dare speak to her for fear of interrupting her trancelike state. Instead she tried imagining the woman somewhere else. It did not work, even though she looked so out of place in this arctic winter landscape. If you saw her with her bluish-violet lips, black skirt, and red low shoes, you might think she was made up and dressed to go to a dinner in the house across the way.

When at midday the pale sun hung in the frosted-glass sky, the trek stopped to feed the horses and warm up a little beside small fires. The Lázár family sat protected from the wind by one of their carts and ate the potatoes that had been cooked the night before. Barely a word was spoken; it was silent save for the whistling of the wind blowing the snow across the plain and the drone of the occasional invisible aircraft scudding above their heads. Nobody looked up; they were all used to this by now. Only the little children began to cry.

In the beginning Lilly had been distressed by how quickly an emergency could become the daily routine. Now she was used to this too, but she sometimes recalled the morning when Lajos had told her that Britain had declared war on Germany. Even back then she was hardly able to believe how quickly the world could get out of joint, how little it needed. Two words were sufficient to change everything, every fruit, every item of furniture or clothing, Lajos, the time, and her body. Now everything was part of a world at war.

Lilly vividly remembered asking what this now meant and Lajos's reply that France would soon follow Britain's example. But that was not what she had been getting at. She realised what the political consequences would be; what she wanted to know was what it meant for their life.

Naturally Lajos was as little able to answer this question as she was. How could he? Even now, five years later, the question could still only be answered partially. The war meant that they had spent the winters at the manor house as well, that their cars were burnt-out wrecks somewhere in the icy wastes of Russia, that they had hidden a persecuted man who was now in a German prison waiting to be executed, that Lajos was chain-smoking and no longer listened to her play the piano.

But she did not know what it meant for their future life. Over the past few years she had learned to take each day as it came and leave all thoughts of the future. There was no point in grappling with the future when the words "It's war!" were enough to turn apples into pears.

The lunchtime break was short, for their progress was slower than that of the Soviet troops and the whole time they had to contend with the fear of being overrun by the front. In addition, when they crossed a railway embankment, a horse pulling the cart in front of them slid on the icy road, the cart overturned, and both wheels on the right-hand side broke. There was no possibility of this vehicle continuing. The trek came to a standstill; the most important luggage was put on other carts and the terrified horses yoked. In this brief interval the people, who before had been walking silently and doggedly in the icy cold, were gripped by a sense of disquiet that became evident in nervous glances at the sky, where the ravens were still circling, and in muttered conversations.

As they moved on, the main topic of discussion was the night and where they might spend it. Unlike the Lázárs, who would stay with aristocratic friends, most had not given any thought to the evening when they set off early that morning. Who knew if they would still be alive? Other treks that had been on the road for longer had been caught up with by the Russians or shelled by aircraft.

The overturned cart seemed to have brought home to them the futility of their undertaking. They were fleeing westwards in a temperature of minus fifteen degrees, without knowing how close the Russians were behind them and how far they would have to go to escape them. Besides, the sun was sinking deeper and deeper without their having spied a church or barn where they could have taken shelter. Eva thought once more of the story of the blind man searching for a house in the endless darkness.

Having sat one of the three dachshunds on his lap so they could warm each other up, Pista wondered how he was going to find Matilda now, with people abandoning everything, entire villages fleeing to the west, and the Russians overrunning the country. Maybe at this very moment she was on her way to the west too.

A scream jolted him from his thoughts—

The young woman was standing beside the light-blue perambulator, ripping her hair out; black tufts lay at her feet. She was not crying and had only screamed momentarily. She was only tearing her hair out, and her whole body was trembling. The trek stopped, but nobody went to her. Bending over the perambulator, the woman took out the child and pressed it to her chest. Only now that he saw the child quite still even though the woman was shaking badly did Pista realise what had happened.

When she collapsed to the ground, an elderly woman tentatively approached her. She removed a fur glove, bent down, and placed a hand on her back.

Any attempt to talk to her was fruitless; she merely kept muttering incomprehensibly. Eventually two men lifted her up and put her on a cart. She would not let go of the child. The light-blue perambulator stayed where it was in the snow.

The house itself was barely visible from the road; only the three drawing-room windows shimmered in the darkness. Just as the life of poor peasants was confined to one room to save on wood, that of the Fekete family had also been restricted to a single room these past few weeks, to avoid signalling their presence to the Russians with too much light. Waiting for them at the iron gate to the drive was a servant who tried to conceal his shivering. Relieved to finally be able to leave his post, he strode ahead to announce their arrival.

A fire was crackling in the drawing room. Its warmth made Pista feel extraordinarily tired. Only now did he realise how much the cold had taken out of him. Exhausted, he dropped onto the sofa and closed his eyes. His fingers hurt, his cheeks were red and hot; he could have fallen asleep on the spot. The voices of his parents and the Feketes sounded like his and Eva's when they used to try to talk to each other underwater in the pool at the manor house. Groggy, he listened to them discuss their options.

"We can't stay here, Péter! You know as well as I do that we need to move further west!" his father said.

"But surely we can wait until morning to fetch the large horse-drawn cart. Riding to the hunting lodge now in the dark would be pointless," Count Fekete replied.

"The Russians are advancing at three times the speed of the treks! Who knows where they'll be in the morning."

"You're right."

Opening his eyes, Pista saw the count stub out his cigarette. At a stroke the tiredness had drained from his body.

"I'm coming with you," he said, getting up.

His father gave him a serious look, then said, "Absolutely not! You need to rest. Besides, we need someone to stay here and look after the women."

Although he did not know how he was supposed to do this, Pista gave a resolute nod. If he could not comfort his sister, then at least he had to protect her.

37.

STILL HALF ASLEEP, HE TOOK THE SHADOW BY THE DOOR TO BE his father. He seemed to be looking for the bed in the darkness of the unfamiliar room, which is why Pista softly cried, "Here!" The shadow jerked its head in his direction and moved away from the wall. From the stiff movements Pista realised that it was not his father.

Before he could sit up, the shadow pushed him into the pillow and switched on the bedside lamp.

He was brandishing a pistol. Apart from this he did not correspond to the image that Pista had of the Russians. Yes, he was dirty and stank of alcohol, sweat, and smoke, but his beard was sparse and his shoulders narrow and bony. Moreover, he was only a year or two older than Pista.

With hand gestures the soldier ordered him to get up slowly. Pista was a full head taller than him and much broader. But what good was this when the other man had a pistol?

He thought about what his father had said to him yesterday evening before he and the count had gone out again into the snow, and about his sister, who was lying at the other end of the room and had not yet been discovered by the Russian.

As if the soldier had read his thoughts, he looked past him, spotted Eva, who was pretending to be asleep, and ordered her loudly to get up and come over. She was wearing a white nightdress, and Pista noticed to his shock that she had developed breasts. Although these were no bigger than plums, the soldier was bound to notice them.

The young Russian led them at gunpoint to the drawing room where the previous evening they had discussed when they thought the Soviet troops might arrive. The first thing Pista saw was his mother. She was sitting bolt upright in a silk-covered armchair and essayed a smile when they entered the room. The soldier instructed them to sit on the sofa where Pista had almost fallen asleep hours before. In the other armchair sat Countess Fekete, who like his mother was wearing a velvet morning coat, but who was completely slumped.

Apart from the two women there was an officer and two other soldiers standing in the room, which had been transformed by their presence. In their filthy uniforms and mud-caked puttees they looked out of place, vaguely reminding Pista of the peasants who came to beg for money. At the same time the countess, Eva, and he had the same submissive, ashamed demeanour as the soldiers. By contrast, none of this seemed to affect his mother. She was sitting as upright as ever, looking neither at them nor at the Russians. In the windows behind her was the night.

"Where are your husbands?" the officer asked so unexpectedly that Eva gave a start. He spoke German but with such a strong accent that it almost sounded like a different language.

"They've gone on ahead," his mother replied coolly in impeccable German.

"They've fled! And left their wives and children behind! Ugh!" he said, spitting on the Persian carpet.

This time the countess gave a start.

As a sign of his humanity and an example of how the Russians were more civilised than the Germans, the officer left the decision of who was going to please him and his men to the countess.

"I have men who have not seen their wives for a very long time. If they are satisfied, I am satisfied. I don't care who satisfies them."

Countess Fekete bent towards Lilly and whispered to her. Then they both got up to go to the kitchen in which Imre and the staff had been locked.

Pista and Eva remained in the drawing room, trying to avoid the soldiers' gaze. Eva wondered, as she had done for weeks, what exactly a rape was. She had never heard the word before, but it was on everybody's lips. It must have something to do with the war, maybe even with the Russians. She understood too that it was a sort of sexual intercourse in which the woman did not love the man. Whether the men loved the women, she had no idea. And yet she was unable to imagine it any other way, for her mother had once told her that people only had sexual intercourse when they loved each other very much. This had made complete sense to Eva, for why else should you wish to see a man naked?

Pista was worried. His eyes flitted restlessly around the drawing room, avoiding those of the others. He could not look at Eva either, for the sight of her only made everything worse. He knew he was unable to protect her, that he must not move a muscle if one of the soldiers decided to take her into the neighbouring room, and he felt unbelievably ashamed of his helplessness, his inferiority, of the fact that there was nothing he could do. The shame was so great that Pista wanted to cry. He was nineteen years old and sitting in his pyjamas before soldiers who were thousands of kilometres from home, had killed people and lost comrades. He was sitting there as an escapee, someone who had never even shot a hare. In Germany, so he had heard, those boys born in 1930 were already learning how to use antitank weapons. They were five years younger than him and only two years older than Eva. And he was sitting here, not daring to move.

At the same time he despised the soldiers for being uncivilised, for the dirt they brought into the house, the stench, their insensitivity and uncouthness. You could see that they no longer had any sense of other people's suffering, that a human life no longer meant anything to them. Pista was full of anger and hatred, and wished them nothing short of death.

* * *

The countess brought her in like a convict. The officer took off his jacket, hung it over a chair, opened his belt pointedly, and disappeared with the girl into the neighbouring room. She was barely older than Pista.

Countess Fekete and Lilly sank into their chairs. They too were filled with shame. They knew it was wrong, knew that they were the target of soldiers' hatred rather than she, who now had to take the blame on their behalf.

The countess had persuaded her, harried her, said that someone had to sacrifice herself or all of them would be given a turn, that the officer had wanted one of the maids. All of them had stared at the floor.

Now they sat there, Lilly, the countess, and the children, avoiding each other's gaze and trying to block out the sounds from the neighbouring room.

After some long minutes—Pista had fixed his eyes on the grandfather clock the whole time—the door swung open and the officer came out with a flushed neck and an open belt. He put his coat back on and another soldier shut the door behind him.

With each one she became quieter, which on the one hand Lilly found reassuring, for she had heard of one woman whose tongue was cut out by a soldier because he was unable to bear her cries. But it also made her despair.

When the last soldier, the young one who had brought them downstairs, left the neighbouring room, the baroness went in. The stench of male sweat was unspeakable. The girl lying on her stomach was whimpering because she thought Lilly was another soldier.

38.

On 23 December, Imre, who was twiddling his thumbs at the window, watched Lajos disappear into the forest. He was wearing a thick knitted jumper and carrying an axe. Beneath his boots the dry twigs cracked and the frozen moss crunched; above him the birds were making no noise and not a breath of air stirred the treetops. Trudging for a long time through the silent forest that felt like an abandoned city, he did not stop until he found a fir tree several heads taller than himself, then gripped the axe with both hands, took a deep breath, and began hitting the tree like a madman, uncoordinated but with every ounce of his strength, so that soon the trunk was covered in deep, pale notches. The rich thudding sound with which the axe dug into the wood travelled through the entire forest. Lajos's muscles were burning, his head glowing and steaming, his cheeks were a feverish red, and he was panting. He put all his dejection, fury, and shame into those axe blows.

When the Christmas tree finally toppled and lay in the needle-covered snow, the baron dropped the axe and dragged the fir with bleeding hands out of the forest.

The days over Christmas were even bleaker than those when the body of the tutor from Vienna had been found. Back then only Ilona had been plagued by feelings of guilt; this Christmas everyone was except for Eva.

Lajos could not get out of his head the image of the Jews walking to the station, Lilly tried in vain to forget the whimpering of the maid, and Pista struggled with the anger he felt at himself for having done nothing, even though he knew that there was nothing he could have done.

After the soldiers had eaten, drunk, and raped, they had set off for the hunting lodge to shoot Count Fekete and Lajos. Fortunately, on their way there, they had received the order to advance north because the Red Army was mustering all its soldiers to encircle Budapest.

Why Pista survived remained a mystery. It must have been the officer's decision not to shoot him. Perhaps Pista had reminded him of his own son; perhaps he had simply become tired of killing.

A bath, not too hot, had been run for the maid, to relieve her soreness and irritated skin. After she had been thoroughly washed, carefully dried, and dressed in one of the countess's silk dressing gowns, she was given a precious ruby ring, which she accepted without any enthusiasm.

When the front line had pushed on towards Budapest, the Lázárs moved back to the manor house even though they expected the Russians to seize it at any moment.

On Christmas Eve, after dining in silence and unwrapping the few presents, Lajos quietly entered the bedroom where Lilly was already asleep. He saw her outline beneath the covers, her hand on the pillow, and her clothes over the back of the chair, for she had forgotten to draw the curtains.

When Pista and Eva had gone to their rooms, he with his books and she with her toys, he had stood up, given Lilly a kiss on her forehead, and left the dining room. She stayed in her chair. He lit a cigar in the smoking room and sat down but, unable to settle, got up again, paced around the room, looked at the hunting scenes, making sure he still found them hideous, stubbed out his cigar, lit another, coughed a few times, opened the door, and saw from Lilly's trembling shoulders that she was crying. He closed it again and stayed in the smoking room until he heard her get up from her chair and go upstairs.

Now she was lying in bed, looking as if she had not only cast off her clothes but also the thirty-two years since he had fallen in love with her. He had not thought in a long time about how they had been in the past. Back then they believed that everything would be fine just so long as they had each other. Now he did not even know if they were still in love. He felt comfortable with her, she was good to him and a beautiful woman, but did he love her? And she him?

He did not know.

But now that she was bathed in the moonlight reflected in the snow, and she resembled the young Lilly Grünfeld, this did not matter. He undressed, hung his clothes over hers, and lay beside her in bed. It had started snowing again. He put his arm around her warm body and watched the large silver snowflakes gently fall through the darkness, burying beneath them all that was alive and all that was dead.

39.

Whilst the lily of the valley with its bowed white heads lined the edge of the forest and the cherry blossom burst open, then withered, making way for the spectacle of the unfurling apple blossom, Budapest lay in rubble and ash. Although the battle for the capital had ended three months earlier, the population had still not recovered from the days of the conquest.

After the counteroffensive by the remaining German and Hungarian troops had failed and the last units surrendered on 13 February, Marshal Malinovsky allowed his men three days of free looting to celebrate the victory. A Hungarian bishop compared the circumstances—similar to how Zuckmayer described the Austrian Anschluss—to hell on earth. Men were abducted, churches destroyed, apartments plundered, the little that remained to eat gobbled up, and women, from twelve-year-old girls to those about to give birth, abused.

At the same time Edmund Pontiller was brought into a barren, windowless room in Munich's Stadelheim Prison, in the centre of which stood a guillotine. The priest was slightly disappointed that the guillotine was at ground level, thereby robbing him of the sensation of rising up to God, setting himself above the heretics and the living, and dying a glorious martyr. The incensed crowd, desperate to tear him to pieces, was missing too. His death would be plain, fast, and meaningless.

As the iron door was closed, he wondered whose lives he had left a mark on, really. He had travelled around a lot, sown doubt about Hitler's Germany in the most varied religious communities, but had never stayed anywhere long enough to not feel lonely anymore or to get to know people properly.

At least he had been right and would ultimately be seen, notwithstanding his death, as a victor. One of those who had not allowed himself to be blinded and carried along, who had been strong and courageous enough to stand up for his faith.

He was taken to the machine that relieved the executioners of work and responsibility and ordered to sit on the wooden bench. He did not create any difficulties, did everything they demanded of him as best he could. He was astonished to find his head preoccupied with trivialities, for he had always thought that your life flashed past you in a moment like this. But he could hardly recall it, as if he had left his past outside, by the heavy iron gate. The person sitting here and the one who had once been a child, a young monk, a priest, and—he could not help but grin when he thought of this term—a resistance fighter did not seem to be the same.

He marvelled at the efficiency of the guillotine, which perfectly reflected the brutality of the National Socialist regime. The coarse, primitive wooden bench, the now slightly blunted blade, the metal bucket into which his head would roll, and the tin chute down which his blood would flow directly into the drain.

As he lay on his stomach, he thought of Eva, who had made him show her his book of Vermeer paintings every day. Maybe she could have freed him from his loneliness, for unlike most people she had seen him as a human being rather than a one-dimensional figure struggling in vain against their time. Hopefully she had found the book that he had stuffed under the mattress even as boots were resounding in the corridor.

One of the attendants stepped up to the guillotine, tied his wrists and ankles to the bench with leather straps, and unfastened the safety catches. Edmund Pontiller closed his eyes—and saw a whole life pass before him, which began with the pain of being refused a goodnight kiss by his mother and concluded with the endless search for lost time.

40.

In mid-June, when the turmoil that had followed the Soviet takeover of power had settled and the first wave of arrests had slackened off, Lajos and Pista travelled to Budapest to repair their damaged house. Pista had insisted on accompanying his father, principally because of Matilda. He was determined to find her and redeem all those future promises that had been contained in their first and only kiss.

The war in Europe was over; the city lay in ruins. Cavernous holes gaped from buildings, through which the rain fell on parquet floors, wallpaper, and carpets, hills of rubble and debris piled up on the edges of streets, and all that remained of the bridges were the pillars that rose from the Danube like menacing memorials.

And so they had to cross the river by boat. Pista looked into the brown water and thought of the thousands of soldiers who had been carried away by the current during the siege.

Only when the boat had almost reached the Buda side did they notice that the spire of the church where they used to attend Sunday Mass was missing. Pista could scarcely believe it—something which had been there all his life, something he had taken for granted, no longer existed. How often had he peered out of the classroom window, wishing that the golden clock hand would move faster! How many nights had he lain awake, waiting for the bells to strike seven, heralding the beginning of a new day when he could see Matilda.

Whereas in the manor house, where he had almost been unable to associate anything with Matilda and thinking of her had occasionally required a real effort, here everything reminded him of her. Every street, every building, every tree, and every pigeon seemed to have something to do with her. With every single thing he glimpsed, the possibility existed that Matilda had seen it too.

On the way from the jetty to her building Pista felt like asking everyone they encountered on the devastated riverbank if they by any chance knew a Matilda. He imagined her coming towards him. Would he recognise her at all? She was, after all, twenty-one years old now, one year older than he. Yes, surely he would recognise her!

All the same, he could not envisage her as a woman. In his mind's eye he only ever saw the girl who had kissed him on the lips outside her building. He was then pierced by the idea, as if by a bullet, that she might have kissed someone else in the meantime. She was an adult now, and, unlike him, who had spent the six years in the isolation of the manor house, she had been living amongst people. Besides, in the war you had no time to think of the past. All that counted was the now, and perhaps tomorrow, which was so uncertain that young people, terrified of dying a virgin, fell on each other behind the bushes in the park. And yet, the idea that Matilda and someone else . . . left him reeling.

Unlike the church, which had been almost completely levelled by artillery fire, only the roof of their house had been destroyed. Nor had it been plundered. Before they could unlock the door and enter, their neighbour came hurrying over to invite them in for a glass of apricot schnapps. Although the two of them were exhausted from the journey, they gratefully followed him—they had not seen one another in years, after all.

They sat down, the maid brought the bottle with the white label and three small glasses, and the neighbour served them.

"The last time I saw you, you were still a boy, and now you're drinking schnapps in the afternoon!" He laughed.

Beginning with the battles, which he described objectively and with precision, he moved via Horthy's wartime government and several glasses of schnapps to the Arrow Cross and their crimes against the Jews.

"Horthy had already rounded them up," he said. "But the real pogroms only began under the Arrow Cross. They shot whole lines of Jews into the Danube, and stormed their hospitals and old people's homes. They killed one hundred and fifty people in Bíró Hospital and transported everyone from the home on Alma utca to Városmajor Park where they slaughtered them all."

Their neighbour had begun to sweat; the bottle of schnapps was empty. He ordered the maid to bring another and three napkins. Then he continued, "But the worst thing is, everybody knew and nobody did anything. Even the Church was in on it!"

The maid brought the bottle; he topped himself up (Lajos and Pista were still on their second glass) and wiped his glistening brow with a napkin.

"There was one priest who was particularly keen on the murder of the Jews. His name was Father Kun. He was a member of the Arrow Cross himself and responsible for hundreds of killings. With his men he would drive them from their homes, even those with letters of protection, stand them by the banks of the Danube or up against a wall, and command, 'In the name of Jesus Christ—fire!'"

For a while they sat facing each other in silence. Pista had never really thought about what his father had done in the war. Of course he realised what area it had been in, but it had never been spoken about. Besides, he had to do it; he'd had no other choice.

"Well, many thanks for your hospitality," Lajos said, getting to his feet while Pista was still pondering the difference between explaining and forgiving a particular action.

41.

The house was empty when Pista awoke the following morning. His father had left early to meet some former business associates in the city centre and find workmen who could repair their roof as quickly as possible, despite the general devastation. Save for the scratching and cooing of the pigeons who had settled in the attic, it was silent in the house.

Although it was only nine o'clock and the sun was barely visible behind a yellow haze, a leaden sultriness weighed on the day, so when he arrived at the jetty, Pista felt as if he were sick with fever, a sticky film of sweat over his skin, hair crumpled and tousled, cheeks and temples glowing, and yet shoulders and the back of his neck freezing.

The cooler air above the water soothed him somewhat, but he could not banish the thought of the bodies floating into the Black Sea.

On the other side of the river he walked, head bowed, past people who were waiting in a cluster to be let onto the boat. Pista crossed the street and a small square with a few benches and trees, and entered a bakery where he bought a poppy-seed roll. Too restless to sit down, he ate it pacing the square. If he kept moving, his thoughts took a pause; if he sat still, they came thick and fast.

Ever since his father had allowed Pista to accompany him on the trip, his mind had been focused on the question of what it would be like when he came face-to-face with Matilda again. He had been longing for this moment for six years—and now it scared him. What if she was engaged? If she no longer remembered him or had changed so much that they no longer had anything to say to each other?

Pista was not aware of how much time had passed, for each day at the manor house had been scarcely different from any other, running on evenly and seamlessly from the last. Only now that he could see the mark it had left on the city, how everything lay in rubble and ashes, not merely the imposing Jugendstil buildings, but also the bridges, the trees in the parks, the streets and social values, did he realise that everything was different. The world in which they had met and taken leave of each other no longer existed.

After eating his roll and drinking some water from the fountain in the middle of the square, he went on. The side streets, not important for the general traffic of the city, were still full of potholes. Men and women worked in the ruins, on the fields of debris and heaps of stones. Pista wandered through the streets without recognising anything. The jetty lay downstream from the monastery school, so he had only a rough idea of where Matilda's building was. As the sun climbed higher, the haze dispersed, but the sky remained milky and deep. Pista was sweating and felt as if he were swallowing dust. The people breaking up stones, shovelling them out of the way, or transporting them on handcarts looked unwelcoming. Pista gained the impression that they had not found their way out of the survival mode they had adopted over the past few years. Still the sole objective seemed to be to get through the day.

Their own existence had been no different; since their flight to the Feketes, they had not recovered their former self-assurance either. They lived in constant fear, and in the expectation that the communists would soon take everything from them and that their return to the manor house would only be of short duration.

At the moment, however, these worries were far away. All he could think about was Matilda.

At the same time he was as receptive to the world as a sick man who, after weeks behind drawn curtains, takes a brief Sunday stroll through the neighbourhood, which is quiet and deserted, yet full of life that flows through him, strengthening him for his ongoing battle with the illness.

He walked slowly through the streets, feeling as if he were on a different planet and imagining their reunion. He had no plan; nor had he given thought to what he would say. He would simply ring the bell and wait for her to look out of the window, recognise him, and come down. How often he had imagined her bedroom! The desk at which she wrote her letters to him. The chair she sat on. The mirror she looked at herself in. The chest of drawers in which she kept objects that meant something to her. The bed in which she slept and dreamed.

He recalled a letter in which she had described a dream—

She was in a fishing village; the waves were pounding the cliffs with such fury that the surf could be heard all over the village as an accompaniment to everything the people did. It was night and had been for a long time, months or years. And it was wartime. The front had been pressing ever farther forward, from inland to the coast. Now it was here, surging against the village like the waves against the shining black cliffs. The village was in complete darkness, in a landscape above which no stars twinkled, by a sea whose blackness was untouched by any moonlight. Enemy soldiers strode through the streets, their uniforms from the nineteenth century, sabres rattling with every step. Matilda was standing on the first floor of a simple fisherman's house, peering anxiously out of the window into the gloomy alley. When another patrol marched past, she turned away and saw that Pista was lying in bed behind her. When she lay down beside him, the soldiers whose footsteps and rattling sabres carried through the wooden walls now seemed far away and utterly harmless.

After roaming the streets for quite a while, from the chaos of which only the occasional familiar building, church, or little park emerged, he gave up his haphazard search and decided to return to the river. From there he would at least be able to find the monastery school, and the building in which Matilda lived would not be far from it.

Once more the water relaxed him, and the sky here also seemed higher and broader, no longer as if it might sink onto the roofs at any moment, crushing everything beneath it.

But he could not get out of his head the images their neighbour had etched into it yesterday. He went upstream along the riverbank, the hills on the opposite side were green, the water flowed slowly, the castle was still standing, despite everything, and all he could think of was how the Jews had been lined up and shot, here, where he was walking.

The sight of the monastery school stirred nothing in him, but no sooner had he left the square between the two school buildings, heading for Matilda's building, than he was overcome by memories. All the emotions he had felt then surged back. He remembered walking beside her, painfully apprehensive that he might say or do the wrong thing, but at the same time deeper in life than ever before. He had picked up on everything—the wind wafting through the dry, bare bushes, the delicate clouds of breath by Matilda's mouth, the smell of snow, candied almonds, and chimney smoke, the brown grass in the park, the park keeper's rough, violet hands, the way Matilda spoke, checking with fleeting sideways glances that he was listening to her—and somehow all of this was woven together.

Pista turned into the street and was relieved to see that all the buildings were still standing, the facades only pockmarked with bullets here and there.

Here he had escorted her home, arm in arm, as the street lamps had come on. He could remember her words verbatim. "When the lamps come on, it always makes me feel wistful," she had said, and at that very moment he wanted only to embrace her and never let go.

Now he was standing outside the door where she had asked him to say her name. How warm he had felt then! He said it; she thanked him and then kissed him—just like that, right on the lips as if this would not change his whole world at a stroke.

As Pista was trying to find the bell with her family name beside it, an elegantly dressed woman stepped out of the building, almost bumping into him. After giving him a suspicious glare, she asked if he was looking for something.

He nodded sheepishly, wiped the sweat from his brow with the back of his hand, and said, "I'm looking for the Telkes family. Specifically their daughter, Matilda Telkes."

As he uttered the name, a shadow darted across the smooth, masklike face of the woman. Pulling a leather handbag in front of her stomach, she said, "The Telkeses don't live here anymore."

Pista nodded, as if he had guessed this. But her words were a blow to the gut.

"Do you know where they live now?" he asked.

The woman shook her head.

He nodded again, crestfallen, but did not let her pass; something about her manner gave him the feeling she knew more.

"Did you know them well?" the woman asked, without looking him in the eye.

Another nod.

She looked up.

"Their housekeeper now works at 24 Váci utca. If you pass by at around eight o'clock, you might be able to talk to her."

He thanked the woman profusely, but she merely pushed past him without another word.

Now the sun stood almost vertically in the sky. Pista decided to look for a restaurant, have a bite to eat, and then consider what to do with his time. He did not want to go back to his own house; it was too big to be there alone. He had no friends in the city, and he could not meet his father either, for he was too busy, and besides, Pista had said yesterday evening that he would be spending the whole day seeing old schoolfriends. In the hope of finding Matilda and having dinner with her, he had also told him that he did not know when he would be coming home, and so his father should go ahead and eat.

Pista found a small beer garden in an inner courtyard nearby, where they served simple Hungarian dishes. He sat at one of the wooden tables with red-and-white check tablecloths and ordered a beer and lángos.

In his mind he tried to capture the moment when the woman's face had darkened, but the longer he thought about it, the more uncertain he became. Was it not just a cloud drifting across the sun? Or had he merely imagined the whole thing?

The waitress brought his beer, gave him a brief smile, and went away again. What was Matilda doing? he wondered. Was she working? Maybe she was studying, or she was a housewife and mother. What did he know? Nothing, he knew absolutely nothing at all!

Finishing the beer in a few gulps, he sensed himself becoming light-headed but ordered a second nonetheless. Again the waitress smiled at him, which pleased Pista but also troubled him, for he would be seeing Matilda again soon; he could not allow himself to feel flattered just because he had been smiled at by some waitress.

He tried to recall Matilda's smile but without success. Instead he was struck by the idea that they might have fled, for why otherwise would their housekeeper no longer be working for them?

The waitress brought his food and gave him another smile that he met with a scowl.

It was not necessarily that; there could be many reasons why she no longer worked for the Telkes family. Perhaps the mother had found out that the housekeeper had allowed them to say goodbye to each other and then dismissed her. Or they had become bankrupt and were unable to afford her any longer. This would also explain why they had moved away. Maybe the father had betrayed the mother with her; these sorts of things happened even in the best families, as his father always said.

Pista stayed sitting there until the courtyard was in shade again and got drunk without having intended to. When he left the beer garden at around three o'clock, he noticed that the heat and alcohol were having a greater effect on him than he had thought. He headed for Andrássy út; he needed more sky above him.

Although he had never cared much for music—unlike with literature and the fine arts he had simply found no connection to it—on his way to the boulevard he felt an overwhelming urge to see the State Opera House. He had always enjoyed sauntering up and down Andrássy út, for this street—and especially the opera house—embodied like nothing else the time of the Monarchy. The buildings were monumental, palatial, old-fashioned, grandiose, and achingly beautiful. But what Pista was most fascinated by, then as now, was the Metró, which moved through the city in its system of tunnels beneath the ground.

When he descended the steps to it, he was delighted by the coolness down there and waited for the yellow headlight eyes to appear in the black of the tunnel. When the train arrived, he got on and remained standing, though he still did not feel completely steady on his legs.

Even the Opera underground station was special, for unlike the other, less impressive ones, it had two rows of columns that were painted brown rather than green. He got out, went up the steps, cursed the heat that instantly enveloped him again, and with his hand shielded his eyes from the smeary afternoon sun.

Whereas music left him cold, the opera house with its neo-Renaissance architecture, balconies, granite columns, and sculptures took his breath away every time. The Liszt statue too, which he now stopped in front of, moved him deeply, even though he did not have a single piece by the composer in his head. For Pista it was not about the music or the man; the indefatigable and glory-seeking genius who, during the time of Lisztomania, as Heinrich Heine called the Europe-wide euphoria for the piano virtuoso, had to kill a dog whose coat was the same colour as his hair so he could satisfy his female admirers' desires by giving them locks, could have walked past him without Pista turning around. What moved him was merely what the Liszt statue guaranteed: a life beyond death.

He had no idea where this fascination came from, but he had long been preoccupied by the relationship of things to transience. He had always been surrounded by death. On the one hand, concrete death, to which his grandparents had fallen victim and which now was not spoken about; on the other, abstract death that included the downfall of the Monarchy, the decline of the aristocracy, and the disappearance of the traditional values on which their world was founded.

Pista spent the rest of the afternoon walking to Hősök tere, Heroes' Square, to sweat the alcohol out of his body, sitting in the shade in the city park, and eventually taking the Metró to Váci utca. When he arrived outside number 24, he was still a quarter of an hour too early, which was why, pacing up and down at the corner, he tried to convince himself that only in the shop window he was now walking past did he look like a madman.

All of a sudden something fell with a thud right beside him on the pavement.

He flinched, letting out a short cry, glanced around anxiously for fear that Matilda might have re-entered his life precisely at this extremely embarrassing moment, and then looked in relief at the thing at his feet. It was a pigeon. He threw his head back and gazed up at the sky, as if expecting to see a dark cloud from which more pigeons would soon come crashing to earth. But the sky was a milky blue and cloudless save for a few smears. There were no more pigeons in sight.

Bending over the bird, Pista saw that it was still alive. It was lying on its side, its red feet tense and tucked up, the wings folded. It had laid its small, round head on the ground; the one amber-coloured eye Pista could see was looking vigilantly at him, without the pigeon making any move to fly away. It was breathing so heavily that its entire body rose and fell, similar to someone bent double and lonely, crying for a loved one in the middle of the night.

As he did not know what to do, unwilling to touch the pigeon because of possible germs it might have, and the church bells were just striking eight o'clock, he left the bird as it was, promising himself that he would attend to it later.

Despite his shirt collar, yellow with sweat, his crumpled jacket, and his nervous demeanour, he was allowed inside; giving his surname was sufficient. Now he was sitting on the only chair in Dora's attic room, waiting for her to come back with the tea, without which she had not wanted to talk. The room was small and sparsely furnished. She placed the teapot and porcelain cups on the bedside table, which she had moved between the bed and the chair he was sitting on, and sat on the bed.

"I remember so well Matilda pestering me every morning and evening to let her speak to you at last. Naturally she knew I couldn't do that; otherwise her mother would have dismissed me on the spot."

Picking up the teapot, she served Pista, then herself, and took a sip. Pista copied her, burning his tongue, and it took all his self-control not to spit the hot tea straight in her face.

"But I could understand the child. Oh, how I could understand! You young people forget that we were young once too. You might not be able to imagine it, but we were also naïve, forlorn, and in love.

That's why in the end I allowed you to say goodbye to each other, but you remember that yourself."

Pista gave a cautious nod. He did not want to interrupt her flow, for she was talking about Matilda, who with every word Dora said was becoming more deeply anchored in the real world from which she had drifted further and further during his years at the manor house, where nobody had known about her.

"The beginning of the war was terrible. Matilda just cried and cried. But over time she got better, began to eat properly again, having allowed herself nothing but semolina pudding for months, and she no longer kept falling asleep at school either. All the same, something had changed, gone awry or been snuffed out. She only ever looked forward to the moment when the street lamps came on; it was the most beautiful moment of the day. The longer the war went on, the quieter she became. Even Mr. and Mrs. Telkes began to worry. Whereas at the start they were convinced that the government wouldn't simply hand over the Hungarian Jews to the Germans, now they had their doubts."

Pista felt sick.

"Is Matilda Jewish?"

Dora looked at him with a mixture of astonishment and sadness.

"You didn't know?"

He shook his head.

"The Telkes family is of Jewish origin. I thought you knew that."

"I never thought about it. I expect I was too busy being in love."

"Probably," Dora said. "Under Kállay life wasn't so bad for them. But when the Germans occupied the country and Sztójay became prime minister, this changed. At the end of March, when the government ordered Jews to wear the star, Mr. Telkes's business was closed down. Their assets had already been confiscated. After twelve years working for them I had to go. Luckily they had just dismissed the Jewish maid in this house. But I missed Matilda, and I was very worried. At the beginning of May Mr. Telkes began queueing outside the Swiss embassy every morning, in the hope of securing three passports. But every evening he would come back with none. In the summer I then met a man who forged letters of protection. And so they got a place in the greenhouse of the Swiss ambassador, Carl Lutz. I visited them there from time to time, bringing them food and chocolate for Matilda whenever I was able to get hold of a piece."

Dora smiled.

"When I still worked for them, every day Matilda would break off a small piece of chocolate in the pantry. She thought I wouldn't notice, but I liked her too much to squeal on her."

Now Pista smiled too, but then asked seriously, "Where is she now?"

Dora looked at her hands, then continued, "On New Year's Eve, at night, an Arrow Cross troop in search of Jews with forged papers stormed the greenhouse. All three of them were shot dead."

Pista gazed at her, but she did not look up. In the sitting room below he could hear voices. Dora's shoulders were quivering. He remembered the pigeon. Getting up, he fastened the button of his jacket and said, "Thank you. And thank you for the tea."

He opened the door, went out, closed it behind him, and stood in the stairwell for a while. Downstairs the voices, behind him Dora's sobbing. He went down and out of the front door without saying goodbye. The pigeon had gone. He wandered through the streets. The people he passed stared at him. I must look like a madman after all, he thought, without realising that tears were streaming down his face.

Fleeing the looks he was getting, he entered a park in which it was dark beneath the dense canopy of its hackberry trees, despite the brightness of the evening sky. He dropped onto a bench, braced his elbows on his thighs, and threw up.

THE SIBLINGS

42.

On one of those rare afternoons without rain in late summer 1948, the crunching of gravel became associated with a feeling of loss, burying itself so deeply inside Pista that he would not be rid of it for the rest of his life. Years later, when he was already living in Zurich, he gave up his first apartment because the bedroom window was above a park with a gravel surface where elderly Italian gentlemen, who had arrived fifty years earlier for the building of the Simplon Tunnel and other major construction projects in Switzerland, played boccia. When it was raked every morning, the sound of the crunching made him so melancholy that he could barely get out of bed.

That afternoon in 1948, Pista was reading as he lay on a lounger by the pool. As the dark clouds had already thinned out in the morning and he did not know what else to do with his Sunday afternoon, he had asked the servant to set up the garden furniture.

His father had wanted to go riding with him, but the fields and meadows were so wet from weeks of rain that the horses would have sunk with every step, while the air was full of midges which would have rushed at them at once.

The effect that the novella had on him was intensified by the damp smell of grass that rose beneath the heavy sun, the warbling of a blackbird that sounded lost in the empty garden, and the still, warm air. The sentiments of the ill-fated Gustav von Aschenbach, renouncing his life and all his values, drifting infatuated and sick through the streets of the decaying city, mingled with his own.

The sudden crunching of gravel made him look up. He was astonished to see not Venice but the surface of the pool. Although his father was at home and they were not expecting visitors, he gave no thought as to who it might be.

But two minutes later the maid came running across the garden towards him, almost slipping on the damp lawn, and said frantically, gasping for breath, "The communists are here! We have to go!"

Pista looked at her as if she had spoken Russian, and so she repeated it even though he had understood. They had been prepared for this, had been expecting it ever since their flight to the Feketes. It nonetheless came out of the blue and hit them like a slap in the face.

Pista got up without saying anything and made for the house as if hypnotised. The two officers were sitting in the drawing room, each with a cup of coffee. They had probably been so brazen as to ask for one.

The men were wearing spotless uniforms, and their expressions seemed to be free of hate or spite. This was certainly not their first expropriation, for the indifference with which they sat amongst all this wealth, which appeared to make no impression on them, must have been down to routine. Or had they, perhaps, simply internalised the communist ideal so fully that luxury no longer meant anything? Pista doubted this, for despite the uniforms, their peasant features suggested that they had spent their lives dreaming of living the sort of life his family had.

They were given an hour to pack. They were not allowed to take the jewellery, silver, or paintings with them. The furniture, the land, and the livestock on it were now the property of the state.

Leaving the officers sitting there, Pista went up to his room and sank onto the bed. Stared at the ceiling. Wondered what to pack. He had so many things—so many that sometimes he thought he would suffocate beneath them all—but most of these objects meant nothing to him. Of significance to him were the forest, the house, the garden, his horse, the library and its books, the piano his mother played, and the fields above which the sun rose and set.

In the corridor outside his bedroom he could hear his family and the servants coming and going in a hurry. All of them were busy packing up as much as possible, trying not to forget anything. He just lay there, staring at the ceiling. Listening to the footsteps, the agitated voices, the warbling of the blackbird.

Ten minutes before they had to leave, he finally pulled himself together, took out his suitcase, and stuffed in it some shirts, suits, trousers, and ties.

Downstairs in the drawing room they had to open their cases again. The officers rummaged with their hands, which Pista found coarse even though they were not, looking for jewellery and other valuables that they could pocket without comment. Finally they asked the baron for his signet ring, which he told them had been lost. Not believing him, they searched his suitcase again and found a precious pair of cufflinks amongst his underpants, which they appeared satisfied with. Lajos had swallowed the ring.

43.

The expropriation had taken place so quickly that it took Pista months to comprehend what had happened. One hour—that was all the state required to take everything away from them.

That same evening they boarded the train for Budapest, sat in silence in their first-class carriage, and gazed out of the window into the ever-deepening darkness. When they got out at the station, the meagre luggage and mild air reminded them that everything was different now. Autumn had not yet begun, and this time they would not return to the house when the primroses began to flower in the city park.

Lilly started to cry as soon as they alighted, in the middle of the platform for all to see. They were embarrassed by this but tried to comfort her as best they could and hold back their own tears.

Pista was not sad, at least not properly so. He knew he ought to be, and pretended he was, but did so only for the others' sake. The expropriation was still so incomprehensible that it elicited nothing more than astonishment in him, and the train journey had seemed like an extended dream.

Now that they were standing on the station concourse, a familiar place, the feeling ebbed. He liked being in Budapest even though the city had no longer been the same since that June evening when he had met with Dora. The sight of its hills, the Danube, the buildings and church towers made him wistful, but at the same time he enjoyed this feeling that kept reminding him of Matilda.

When they entered the dark house, turned on the lights, and pulled the covers off the furniture, still Pista felt nothing. Like Imre he sat in a chair in the drawing room, fixed a point on the wall, and did not take his eyes off it until he went to bed. There he lay awake until morning.

They understood what the expropriation really meant only when they realised they would now have to look for work. The estates they had managed no longer belonged to them, their livestock had been taken away, and the combustion engine factory had likewise been nationalised.

Thanks to his numerous contacts, Lajos soon got a good job in a textile factory and Pista a traineeship at a prestigious insurance company, but they were not happy with their professions. They missed the personal connections, the peasants who had worked for them and respected them, the place where they had spent the major part of their lives. They missed the manor house.

A few days after the expropriation, Lajos had rung his sister in America. No sooner had he told her the bad news than she began to sob, which irritated him for several reasons. First, because Ilona had never liked the manor house; on the contrary, she had always wanted to put it behind her. Second, because the three-minute connection to the US cost a mountain of money which was being wasted on her howling. Third, because she was so far away and her weeping was being conveyed to him across deep-sea cables thousands of kilometres long. And finally, because the whole time he imagined that in some central office of the ÁVO—the secret police—some officer was feeling deeply embarrassed as he listened to Ilona crying and crying.

As they gradually became accustomed to their new life, the thought of officers listening in proved to be persistent. It refused to leave Lajos's head. In every passerby, behind every look he encountered, he suspected an informer. He believed all his colleagues and the workers at the textile factory to be, without exception, communists.

The expropriation had shaken him and made him ripe for such paranoia, but it was fuelled by the seemingly arbitrary arrests to which the family's friends, acquaintances, and neighbours fell victim.

On an evening after another acquaintance had disappeared, Lilly found Lajos lying under their bed. She screamed because she thought he had suffered a heart attack. But he was searching for hidden microphones.

"You're seeing ghosts," Lilly said.

But the baron was firmly convinced that their apartment was bugged and they were being listened to. As a consequence he avoided saying anything political, put a finger to his lips the moment anyone expressed a hint of criticism at the dinner table, and would even drop the odd compliment—loudly, clearly, and without any context—in favour of the government or the Soviet Union. He also bought a copy of *The Communist Manifesto*, which every evening, as soon as Lilly was in bed, he would fetch from the hatrack and place on the chest of drawers by the front door so that the ÁVO officers would see it at once if they rang the bell in the middle of the night. In the morning he would hide it beneath the hats again so that his family did not see what an opportunistic coward he was.

Those arrests that took place at night, when officers got people out of bed, always followed the same pattern. A black GAZ-M20 would arrive; two men in blue uniforms got out, rang the bell, entered the house or apartment, led somebody out, and drove off. Ten minutes, this is all it took the state to make people disappear.

44.

When, three years later, a gleaming black Pobeda actually did stop outside the house, the *Manifesto* was not on the chest of drawers. Nor was it night-time, but a bright morning in March. And thus Lilly, who had not seen the car, got a thorough shock when she opened the door and saw two officers standing there. People had said they always came at night.

One of the officers, a tall, slim man with rimless spectacles who looked more like an intellectual than an armed enforcer of the political police that Rákosi, the dictator, lovingly called the party's fist, said after a curt greeting, "You're familiar with this procedure, Mrs. Lázár. You have to be out of here in twenty-four hours. We are now going to do a brief tour of the house and make an inventory of the furniture and objects of value. At this time tomorrow you will be collected and taken to a farm in the east of the country, though I don't know exactly where. Mr. Imre Lázár, who, if I have read the documents correctly, is insane, will be taken care of. He will be placed in a psychiatric institution."

Lilly felt the blood drain from her face. Holding on tightly to the chest of drawers she thought of all those occasions when she had said something negative about the regime. Had they been careless? Had Lajos been right after all? Or did everybody's turn come sooner or later in such a system, such a society?

"And then?" she asked when she had found her voice again.

The officers looked at her blankly.

"What do you mean, 'And then?'"

"What's going to happen to us? On the farm?"

"Nothing. You'll learn what it means to work and serve the people."

Lilly felt like throwing up. She wanted nothing more than to vomit all over the officer's shiny boots and blue trousers. Ever since they lost the manor house, she had felt nauseous even just hearing the words "bread," "work," and "revolution."

While the officers went through the house, Lilly rang Lajos and Pista at work. It was ten o'clock; they had to be out of here in twenty-three hours. In twenty-three hours they would be aristocrats without a property who would have to work in the fields somewhere in the east until their spines were so crooked and bent that they could see nothing but their own feet.

When Lajos came home forty-five minutes later, the first thing he did was to take the *Manifesto* out from beneath the hats and into the drawing room, open one of the tall arched windows, and hurl the book into the Danube. Lilly, who was sitting on the sofa with a red face and tear-stained eyes, looked at him aghast. Without explanation the baron went into their bedroom and rummaged in the casket containing his jewellery, which since the expropriation of the manor house he had hidden in a place that not even Lilly knew. It was fortunate that he had kept only a fraction of his jewellery at the manor house, but he was faced with the same problem again.

As the officers had not found the casket, the question now was where to put it. Lajos contemplated burying it in the park behind the garden, but then remembered the tens of thousands of people who had died in the battle for the city and who had been hastily interred in the parks, and so discarded his plan for fear of unearthing human bones. He could not take the rings, watches, and cufflinks to a friend either, as his friends were without exception either aristocrats or industrialists, who sooner or later would be expropriated and banished themselves. Besides, the officers were bound to be suspicious if they found no valuables whatsoever.

The only course of action left to him was that which he had used during the first expropriation: swallowing. He recalled with great displeasure poking around in his own shit for his father's gold signet ring, but the swallowing itself had been remarkably easy, which is why he was confident that he could now send larger and chunkier pieces of jewellery down his gullet.

The Lázárs spent the afternoon sitting quietly in the drawing room, staring into space. What would they have talked about? Daily life, which until just a few hours earlier had still seemed important, something that they could worry about, had at a stroke lost all its importance, and the everyday words they were familiar with and which might have offered some consolation were too banal to capture the situation. For they were not sad, angry, anxious, or shocked; their emotions went far beyond these.

Dinner was only less silent on account of the clatter of cutlery and the chewing. It occurred to Pista that this must be similar to the atmosphere at the Last Supper when Jesus announced that someone at the table would betray him.

After dinner, they went to bed out of sheer habit and in the hope of being able to maintain at least a modicum of normality. They did not sleep.

45.

Every morning during the winter months, Eva had to decide between the cold and his hard penis. Early in the morning, when it was so icy in the room that they could see their breath, for the stove that stood between the bed where their parents slept and the mattress she shared with Pista was no longer lit, the only thing that prevented them from starting the day frozen to the core was to warm each other up. But if Eva snuggled up to Pista, he got an instant erection.

She did not know if he noticed it, if when she shifted over to him, he woke up and tried in vain to suppress his body's reaction; they never spoke about it.

Eva did not hold it against him. She knew that there was nothing he could do about it and that the arousal had nothing to do with her personally, only her body. Human beings had their needs, and here on the farm it was not easy to satisfy them.

In all likelihood Pista had not slept with a woman since their expulsion, for unlike her he avoided the peasant women and those who worked in the fields from the nearby village. In truth she had no idea if he had ever had sexual intercourse; she had not heard of any girl. She was seven years younger than he, and had not been interested in such things for long.

Until a year ago she had only been afraid of it. For her, a penis had not been an object of desire but the epitome of evil, pain, male dominance. A major reason for this must surely have been the look on the face of the Feketes' violated maid, which she had never forgotten.

This changed when they were banished a year ago, which was down partly to the young man with the olive eyes and partly to her parents.

What the young man had to do with it can be quickly explained. Like Pista he was probably in his mid-twenties, had black hair, broad shoulders, muscular arms, and narrow eyes, dark as black olives. His name was Milan, and during those months when they had to work in the rice fields, she saw him every day. Sometimes, on particularly hot days, he would take off his shirt and place it around his shoulders. His skin was tanned, and, together with his black hair and dark eyes, it gave him a Mediterranean look.

Her parents' role in helping her discover her sexuality was more peculiar—

Since those crisis years following Pista's birth they had slept with each other almost every day. They themselves were surprised at how great their mutual desire was after all these years and how unaffected their love life was by the madness of their time. Whether the Nazis or communists ruled the country, whether they were in the manor house, Hévíz, or in their Budapest house, whether Lajos came home from the combustion engine factory or the textile factory, most nights they made love.

Not even their expulsion to the farm, where they had to share this tiny room with nothing other than a double bed, a mattress on the floor, and a cupboard, had changed this aspect of their life. The sleep that overcame their children the moment they lay down, utterly exhausted after a day working in the field, provided enough privacy for them. But sometimes Eva, who slept more lightly than Pista, was woken by the creaking of the bed and the moaning of her parents.

The room was so dark that Eva could not even make out the contours of her parents, and it was not hard for her to imagine that the sounds were coming from Milan and her. Sometimes her mother and father whispered to each other, but most of the time they just made animal noises that she could hardly believe were coming from them. When they fell silent, Eva would slide into dreams in which she was always lying beside Milan.

* * *

Whereas the days in the rice fields were torture for the others, Eva enjoyed them. Although the work was hard—the green seedlings had to be transplanted by hand from the dry seed bed into the flooded rice field, and the ripe yellow plants were cut with sickles, bundled on the spot, and then threshed—so long as she could see Milan's head bob up and down or his muscular back, so long as the sky was steel-blue, reflected with aching beauty in the fields that lay underwater, and she could listen to the women from the village talk about their (mainly useless and hard-drinking) husbands, she was content.

She did not miss the school she had just managed to finish in Budapest. Moreover, she liked the "simple" people from the village, who were anything but simple. They might not read as much as she had done and had spent less time at school, but they were not stupid as a result.

Unlike the city folk, who had distanced themselves so much from the origins of life and from their bodies that the sight of the expansive sky above a field or of a corpse laid out in an empty room smelling of flowers and ethanol made them feel uneasy, they, who still worked with their bare hands beneath the sun, had a more direct access to existence.

For this reason Eva was not particularly surprised when, one evening after work, Milan took her aside and asked her if she would like to sleep with him behind the barn. A year earlier she would have slapped anyone who dared ask her so shamelessly if he could deflower her. But Milan's request was so unemotional and he looked at her with such open olive eyes that she could not be angry at him. Besides, through working in the fields she had discovered a pleasure in her own body.

Until now she had regarded this body as a necessary evil that carried out the orders of the mind and was subordinate to it. But now that she barely used her head, needing to do neither arithmetic nor any writing, only bending down, straightening up, bending down, straightening up all day long, she had realised that the body can probably get by better without the mind than vice versa. For what is a genius with an ailing lung or a tumour in the chest? Ill, that is what, nothing more.

Even a painful toe makes it difficult to follow an idea through several stages, let alone compose a piece of music or write a great novel. Living with a limited mind, by contrast, was easy, perhaps even easier than living with a capacious one.

The further the day with its meditative labour progressed, the more Eva's thoughts stole away from her and took on a life of their own. Usually they would then focus on their favourite topic: Milan. They encircled him, his body, his voice, his fluid movements. They undressed him and wandered down his spine, scaled his elbows, and battled their way through the thicket of his pubic hair. She imagined him kissing her neck, her collarbone, her breasts, slipping the blouse from her shoulders, and pushing up her skirt.

Her thoughts knew no limits, and once they had eluded her, it was almost impossible to catch them again. Often the only thing that helped was going to the shed at the edge of the field in the shade of an oak where she, breathing shallowly through her nose, slid her hand down into her skirt.

That evening she gave Milan a searching look—he held her gaze—and nodded slowly. Then she followed him behind the barn.

46.

A WHILE AFTER EVA HAD SEX FOR THE FIRST TIME BEHIND THE barn, on the wooden wall of which the flies warmed themselves in the evening sun, an elderly man, feeling the dizziness that came on every evening and was made worse by the storm clouds rolling in from the east, was looking for Gogol's *Dead Souls*.

He had been searching for the book since hearing the first rumbling of thunder. Given that his library contained twenty thousand volumes, it was not surprising that he could not find the book immediately. And yet, in the past he would have found it more quickly. His memory was on the wane; every day he had to be reminded of things he had always known.

When the distant thunder tore him from his sleep late that afternoon, he had suddenly remembered reading that book as a sixteen-year-old. At the time he was still living in Gori, and he was convinced that nobody had ever written anything better.

Now, looking for it almost sixty years later, he could barely recall the plot and the characters. He also had health problems, suffering from arthritis and arteriosclerosis. At night his joints ached so badly—especially those in the fingers and toes—that often he lay awake for hours. In the daytime it was better, and he could catch up on the sleep he had missed, which is why he was forever prolonging his afternoon rest on the rose-pink sofa.

He knew that the question of his succession was in the air and that his comrades, who appeared so loyal, were merely waiting for him to die. But he did not intend to make it easy for them. They underestimated him, as everybody had done throughout his life.

* * *

He moved on to the next shelf. It could not be that difficult, seeing as he had organised his library alphabetically. It was getting dark outside, which was in part due to the clouds that had now reached the sky above the extensive garden. He thought of the Jewish doctors whose arrest and torture he would order at the end of the year.

He had always been mistrustful—it was impossible to remain at the top for so long otherwise—but age had made him downright paranoid. He no longer trusted anybody, not his servants and bodyguards, nor his doctors or comrades-in-arms, indeed, not even his wife and daughter.

When it was so dark that he would have had to turn on a light to continue his search for this book from his youth, he decided to go to bed and ask somebody about it tomorrow.

Leaving the library, he went into the bathroom, undressed, put on the short pyjama bottoms and vest in which he slept, cleaned his large yellow teeth, and thought of his mother, whom his father had always beaten.

Then he went back into the small dining room where he also slept at night, lay down on the rose-pink sofa, and, just as he was about to turn off the light, saw *Dead Souls* lying on the bedside table.

47.

If, after work, she stood behind the barn, her back against the rough wooden wall, looking at the languid flies, she sometimes remembered with a smile the words of her mother, who had said that people only had sexual intercourse when they loved each other very much. She knew by now that this was not true, that the sexual act was something far too pragmatic and physical to be tied to love.

Had anybody known about her and Milan and asked her if she loved him, she would have said no straightaway. He was too handsome, too immaculate, to be loved by her.

Had anybody seen her behind the barn and asked if she was in love with him, she would have hesitated, rocked her head from side to side, given the question some thought, and then likewise said no.

Since she was sleeping with him she had become more confident, as if she had needed to know she was desirable to feel she had a right to exist. Sometimes she wondered if Milan felt the same way. She doubted it. He moved through life with a self-assurance that seemed to come from inside himself alone.

But Eva knew that she also had a connection to his world, to the way he lived. He had never moved, never possessed anything that could have been taken away from him, had only been to Budapest twice, only ever worked for other people, and was certain that it would remain that way.

At the same time he was a young man who could do as he pleased, who did not have to fulfil any expectations and could marry any woman in the village.

When, with his salty taste in her mouth, she watched him ride home on his red bicycle, she thought that he was very fortunate—and probably did not know it.

48.

Although he was used to the Georgian wine that, despite the moderation advised by his doctors, he drank in copious quantities, he felt very drunk when he accompanied his guests to the door at four o'clock in the morning. He felt nauseous and dizzy, saw his comrades' faces double, and his head felt as if it might burst at any moment.

They put on their coats and took their leave. He gave them deliberately firm handshakes so they would not notice his exhaustion. They were merely waiting for his death, he thought as he crushed their hands. They are merely waiting for your grip to go limp, the iron grip of steely Stalin, and then their time will begin.

Nine hours later, around one o'clock in the afternoon, the bodyguards in the staff quarters were conferring about what to do. Normally Stalin got up around midday, no matter how late he had gone to bed and how much wine he had drunk. But today nothing had stirred behind the window of his dacha, and he had not called for anyone either. Despite this, nobody dared check; an awkward interference in his personal sphere could mean death.

At around nine p.m. Lieutenant Colonel Lozgachev and his superior, Colonel Starostin, argued about who should check that everything was in order.

"You're the superior officer; you should go," Lozgachev said.

Colonel Starostin, who had become paler with every passing hour, shook his head vigorously.

"That's not right," he said. "You have to go."

"What do you think I am? A hero?" Lozgachev said.

Starostin looked over at the dacha. The light had been turned on in the small dining room three hours ago, but otherwise there had been no movement.

His fingers trembling, the colonel offered Lozgachev a cigarette and said, "Let's devise a plan," as if they were about to discuss an important battle.

By ten p.m. they had smoked the entire packet and still had no plan. Colonel Starostin, holding the mail that had been brought from the central committee, then had a brainwave that would rescue them from their dilemma—

One of Lozgachev's duties was to bring Stalin his post. He should enter the dacha under that pretext and check if everything was alright.

Pressing the mail to his chest with sweaty hands, the lieutenant colonel wandered the short distance to the dacha and entered it tentatively, making as much noise as possible to avoid catching the owner unawares.

The hallway and most of the rooms were in darkness; the only light on was in the small dining room. Lozgachev went cautiously, accompanied by the fear of Stalin emerging from thin air and overpowering him.

He enters the dining room—and freezes in horror.

The immortal, in his short pyjama bottoms and vest, is lying on the rug in front of the sofa. He is unable to speak, but he is conscious. Beside him is a book and on the bedside table a bottle of mineral water. There is a dark patch on his pyjama bottoms; Stalin has wet himself.

The bodyguards laid Stalin on the sofa in the large dining hall as it was airier in there. Lozgachev kept watch, still clutching the post.

At around seven o'clock in the morning five doctors finally arrived after the leading functionaries, who had been drinking with Stalin until late the previous evening, had come and gone again without leaving clear instructions.

The doctors' hands were shaking so badly that they could not even unbutton the shirt that had been put on the immortal one. Nor were these specialists, but dentists, surgeons, or general practitioners. The specialists were Jews and, as had been ordered, were being tortured in prison.

Stalin's eyes were closed. He could hear the doctors' whispered words without understanding what they were saying. In his mind he was still lying on the rug in front of the rose-pink sofa, the copy of Nikolai Gogol's *Dead Souls* beside him. And as the voices faded ever further into the distance, as he sank ever deeper into the pillows, he remembered word for word the puzzling end of this novel he had read in his youth.

49.

When, under Imre Nagy, who had replaced the dreadful Rákosi as prime minister, the aristocracy was permitted to return to the cities in late-summer 1953, the delight of the Lázárs (apart from Eva, who would miss Milan and the simple life of the farm where nothing counted but the present) was huge.

But the disappointment that hit them when they arrived in Budapest was even greater—

The city, which at the time of their expulsion had still been trying to resist communist rule, no longer existed. Stalin had throttled it until it had stopped breathing.

Although a different era would dawn under Khrushchev and the new Hungarian prime minister, there was no plan to restore the feudal structures. After all, Imre Nagy had carried out the land reform in the course of which the aristocracy and large landowners had been expropriated.

Their Budapest house thus remained state property, and so the Lázárs had to rent an apartment. This was close to the former Jewish quarter; from the parents' bedroom window you could see the ghetto wall that had not been fully torn down. Beneath the apartment was a small grocery run by a Turkish man whose forefather had fought against Hayo Lázár in the Siege of Szigetvár.

To get to the apartment they had to go through the dusky shop, its shelves full of watermelons, dates, baclava, and other Turkish pastries. At the end of the narrow rows of shelves was the damp stairwell with the rotten banister.

The apartment consisted of a tiny entrance area, a kitchen, a connecting room that was so narrow it barely warranted the description "room," and the parents' bedroom. The connecting room was just big enough to house a sofa for Eva to sleep on. Pista slept in the kitchen, which is why he always smelled of frying oil and fat.

At four o'clock in the morning he would fold up his camp bed, push it beneath the kitchen table, wash in the mouldy bathroom at the end of the corridor that they shared with the building's other residents, get dressed, and go to the bakery where he worked in the mornings.

For three hours he would roll out dough and put bread in the oven. Then he would take off his apron, dust the flour from his clothes, and go to the chemical laboratory where he worked for the rest of the day.

Lajos worked for the post office, during the morning as a postman and afterwards as a postal sorter. The shame he felt at having to earn his money as a postman was so great that his round through the neighbourhood was a daily walk through hell. The sorting work was done in the basement of the post office, which meant that in the darker months of the year, when the sun rose only after he had completed his round, he was as pale as he had been at birth.

In such circumstances it was no wonder that Lajos became depressed. But the past was as responsible for this as the present—

Every evening when pulling down the roller blinds, he saw the wall of the ghetto. Every evening he was reminded of the Jewish funeral procession in Pécs.

Whereas all these years he had justified his behaviour during the war and always invoked Edmund Pontiller, now that he had lost everything despite his efforts, he saw that there was no excuse for what he had done. He was no better than those opportunists who, after the extension of Soviet rule, now professed to be staunch communists. After all, he had placed the *Manifesto* on the chest of drawers by the front door.

The disappointment at their new life in the city edged so slowly into depression that for a long time Lajos did not realise what was happening to him. It was only one evening when Lilly kindly asked him to wash before coming to bed that he realised how long it had been since he last took care of himself, and how much time and effort this required.

In the bathroom other things came to mind that he had been neglecting recently. For example, he had hardly eaten, never laughed, and he was skipping the weekly meetings with other dispossessed aristocrats. But identifying his feelings changed nothing of this; he continued to drag himself through everyday life full of shame and gravity.

Eva understood her father and yet she despised him. Instead of looking forwards or coming to terms with his new life, he was simply giving up as if he were the only one suffering. As if he were the only one who had lost anything.

She, on the other hand, resisted and protested against the system by reading proscribed books by Kafka, de Beauvoir, and Woolf. Every Thursday and Saturday she also went to the "Cellar."

The Cellar was where young aristocrats gathered to smoke, dance, play bridge, and talk. Conversation mostly revolved around the banned books they would swap, or how to topple the regime.

The secret meetings were organised by János, Pista's best friend, who also owned the cellar room. János earned his living as a stuntman, which is why he always had a stock of good stories. His most daring stunt had been a leap from the Chain Bridge in which he had almost drowned and his horse actually had.

Eva spent her days reading. She would have loved to have studied, but as an aristocrat she was forbidden from doing so. Books were thus her university, with Simone de Beauvoir and Virginia Woolf her favourite professors. These two women seemed to understand her like no-one else, and at the same time see through the construct that was the world.

She could have happily had de Beauvoir's words "One is not born, but becomes a woman" etched on her skin. This was another reason she despised her father: because he at least was able to live in this system as a man, whereas she, as a woman, had a more difficult time of it. For even under communism, where all people were supposed to be equal, the talk was only ever of male workers, while those who were women were valued far less. But even more than *The Second Sex* Eva liked *A Room of One's Own*, which she read on a sunny bench one September afternoon. When she shut the book and looked up for the first time in hours, she was a new woman.

50.

Ever since her brother first brought Ákos along to the Cellar and introduced him as "the new Petőfi," Hungary's national poet, Eva had been doing all she could to read something by him. Ákos was the only writer she knew, and although he had not been published, Pista kept assuring her that this was because of the censorship rules rather than the literary quality of his work.

Pista and Ákos knew each other from the national service they had been obliged to carry out for the past six months. As aristocrats they were not permitted to serve as regular soldiers but had to work in a coal mine that was teeming with scrabbling rats the size of puppies.

At weekends they were allowed back home, and sometimes Pista managed to lure Ákos from his desk to the Cellar, for which he had to muster all his powers of persuasion, seeing as the young Petőfi was working on his first great novel that told of the endless stream of time.

Ákos had blond hair—which like Pista's was shaved because of their work in the mine—dark eyebrows and a dark moustache, prominent ears, and sad green eyes that always avoided the gaze of others, but bored through you as soon as you looked away. He was quiet and shy, only contributing to group conversations with a nod of agreement or a laugh. He did not smoke but occasionally drank so much that Pista had to take him home.

Eva found him rather sinister—and yet she wanted to get to know him better, which was not easy because he scarcely gave anything of himself away, out of fear of making himself look ridiculous or being judged. He did not let anyone read his writing either; only once had he recited one of his poems to Pista in the darkness of the mine, which led the latter to the firm conviction that the young writer had a great future ahead of him.

Ákos himself was far less sure. Essentially he regarded what he wrote as poor. He had already thrown his first short novel into the Danube in frustration. Despite this, he wrote like a man possessed, several hours a day, writing even after his shifts in the coal mine in the hope that at some point he would put down something on paper he was satisfied with, and which would endure.

Eva wanted to read some of his work too, because since finishing Woolf's *A Room of One's Own* she had been thinking a lot about women and literature. Unlike Woolf, however, she was less interested in women writers per se and more in the relationship between writers and their female characters.

Kafka, for example, often portrayed his female characters based on an image of women that contradicted the general male viewpoint. But this did not mean that he represented them in a more positive light. The women he described were physically superior to his male protagonists, even violent, and overall he depicted them rather unflatteringly.

At times Eva wished she had been born fifty years earlier and in Prague so she could have met this pale, thin man with the dark eyes and prominent ears in person, learned how he behaved towards women in real life, and seen whether this had anything to do with his portrayal of female characters.

In Ákos she had now been presented with the first opportunity to forge a connection between real life and literature—if only she could have read some of the novel he was working on.

51.

WHAT ELSE DOES A WRITER DO, EVA THOUGHT, THAN STRIP from their characters the right of self-determination? The writer confronts them with wars, gives them depression, or tears away their first love. A power imbalance between perpetrator and victim, albeit only in fiction. The characters cannot fight back; the writer does with them as he or she pleases, allows them to suffer and go on hoping in vain, in order to affirm his or her superiority.

Ákos did not appear to Eva to be someone who was set on determining other people's destinies. He was too shy for this, too decent and too chaste as well.

Unlike the other young men, especially those who, like he and Pista, had been in the mines and lost their senses at the sight of a mere female collarbone or a bare shoulder, he seemed not to have any interest in women.

He never foisted himself on her, never stared directly at her, never peered at her cleavage and never once had he placed his hand on her forearm. And yet she was so blatant in seeking out his company that one night, on the way back through the empty streets to their tiny apartment, Pista asked her if she was in love with Ákos.

"I just find him interesting," she said.

"Finding someone interesting and being in love with them is the same thing," Pista said.

Eva laughed and wondered whether he might be right. Was she indeed in love with him? Was this the actual reason for her approaches, and her literary interest just an excuse? Then she said, "I don't know any other writers; that's the only thing that makes him interesting."

* * *

János and the others, by contrast, found Ákos such a boring individual that not even the fact that he wrote could endear them to him. They only tolerated Ákos in their company because Pista stuck up for him so fervently. Had his books been published or circulated clandestinely by students and aristocrats who opposed the system, at least they could have basked in his reflected glory. As things stood he was just another dispossessed aristocrat who worked in a mine, mourning the old days as they all did, even those who looked to the future, certain that at some point—when the people had had enough of permanent surveillance, the miserable planned economy, the fear of being picked up by a black Pobeda and tortured in the basement of the ÁVO, of the lie that everybody was equal under communism—the regime would be toppled or would destroy itself in its megalomania. Even those who had not lost hope were not in fact hoping for the future, but for the return of the past.

This is why they placed so much emphasis on behaviour, turns of phrase, clothing, manners, and seals, with which they could distinguish themselves from the normal people. They sat in their small, shabby apartments and taught their children how to eat without dropping the books that were clamped beneath their armpits. They bought any old portraits of ancestors depicting people who had never belonged to the family and hung these on the few walls of their apartments. The women wore discreet colours and avoided anything "too": too-deep necklines, too-high stilettos, and too-gaudy lipstick.

If the young children who belonged to that first generation unable to recall a life in a manor house complained about the strict rules of etiquette that were completely out of step with the simple lives they led, their parents would give them a proper smack and say, "This is your capital. When we get our estates back you will be grateful to us!"

52.

When Eva arrived in the Cellar later than usual one evening in early October 1956, Ákos was already rather drunk. He was sitting in the corner of the low-ceilinged room, following a game of bridge without playing himself. In his hand was a champagne glass filled with Unicum, and when he saw Eva, he gave her a candid smile.

He looked better than a year and a half earlier when Pista had first brought him here. As they had finished their national service in the coal mine, he was now wearing his hair longer again and combed back. He was also not as thin or pale.

Eva gave a restrained smile back and sat down with Pista and Kati, who were talking to some other regulars; she did not want them to see how interested she was in Ákos.

Kati, who looked as if she had sprung from an advertising hoarding and was always the most elegant person in the room, no matter where she went, was Pista's first love since Matilda. Although he often thought of her still, wondering what she would look like now aged thirty, what she would have been like as a grown-up woman, as a mother, at some point he had decided that he could not grieve for Matilda forever.

Kati was so different from Matilda that he could not possibly compare them, and this was also the prerequisite for his being able to love her. Although he desired and worshipped Kati more than he loved her. He adored her flawlessness, her style, and her charm. He likewise adored her soft skin, blonde hair, small, firm breasts, and her ears. But he was not familiar with anything beneath this surface. It was not that he did not like her personality or that they were arguing all the time, far from it. It was just that he did not know everything beneath the surface well enough, did not feel it deeply enough to be able to become attached to it. If the form of her ears had been in any way changed, he would have cried out. If, on the other hand, her personality had been swapped for another, he would have been less decisive.

As so often, they were discussing the government and what could be done about it. Ever since Imre Nagy had been deposed eighteen months earlier and replaced by the loyal party man Hegedüs, the situation in the country had deteriorated again. Everybody knew someone who had been interrogated for no reason by the ÁVO. They had even detained János overnight, attempting to force him to a confession with burning cigarettes and electric shocks.

The longer the evening went on, the more inebriated Ákos became. Unlike Pista, who was loud and cheerful when he drank too much, the young Petőfi became tired and sorrowful. Eva had seen this a few times; it was as if the sadness in his eyes spread throughout his entire body. When Eva sat beside him, he did not even look up.

For a while they sat next to each other in silence. Eva watched the others dance; Ákos stared at the green baize.

Eventually Pista came over to them, put a hand on Ákos's back, and said to Eva, "Could you do me a huge favour and take our Petőfi home? Kati's sister is not in tonight, which means we have the room to ourselves!"

Eva nodded. Ákos was so exhausted and drunk that she was not going to be able to find out much about his novel, but perhaps this was her chance to get to know him better.

It was cold outside. The wet asphalt and brown leaves shimmered in the pools of light from the street lamps. Eva's high-heeled shoes echoed in the empty streets. It was as if they were the only people in the city.

Occasionally they turned a corner and caught sight of the castle, towering over the city on the other side of the river. Ákos stumbled once on the kerb; otherwise it was not noticeable that he was drunk. Pista had briefed her about this while putting on his coat.

"If you don't know him, you can't tell that he's drunk. He behaves as normal, walking upright and straight; he doesn't slur his words and isn't rude to people. But he becomes totally disoriented. He doesn't know where he lives or where he is. He would never admit it; he's far too ashamed. He would rather spend the entire night walking round in circles."

Now he was walking right behind Eva, just a pace, so he could see the way she went. Although Eva realised this, she did not say anything.

They wandered silently through the pools of light from the street lamps and vanished into the darkness again. Their footsteps echoed in the empty streets. They were the only people in the city.

Ákos lived in a single room belonging to an apartment, but which could be accessed directly from the stairwell. He opened the door with a steady hand, invited Eva in, and offered her a glass of water. Eva declined graciously and looked around while he sat on the bed and took off his shoes, an act that had something strangely intimate about it.

The room was furnished in a spartan manner and reminded her of the one on the farm. For a moment she felt a yearning to be back there, not in Milan's arms, not beneath the expansive sky or behind the barn, but back in that tiny room where the four of them had lived together. What nostalgia made you miss!

Above the bed hung the portrait of a young man with bare shoulders and a string of pearls around his neck. With its broad brushstrokes the picture was somewhat reminiscent of a Cézanne. Beside the window stood a simple desk that was covered in written sheets of paper, photographs, and books.

When Eva was sure that Ákos had taken off his shoes, she looked round at the bed and saw that he was asleep. He had hung his jacket over the bedpost, but kept on his shirt, tie, and trousers.

It was strange but lovely in a way to be standing in this unfamiliar room, watching this man she barely knew anything about as he slept. She heard him breathing and water flowing in the pipes in the walls. On the desk were the texts she had always wanted to read. She knew he would not wake up, would never find out, and she gazed at his face. He had two small moles, situated symmetrically under each nostril, and his left eyebrow was adorned by a fine scar. When he was asleep, he looked like a child.

She left the room without having read a word. Outside it smelled of snow.

53.

One week later Ákos gave Eva a bag of caramelised almonds. Having bought them that morning, he had carried them around all day wondering whether he should give them to her or not.

When they arrived at the Cellar almost simultaneously and took off their coats, he handed her the bag, mumbling that he was sorry and felt dreadfully embarrassed.

"You don't have to be," Eva said, after thanking him. "Even when you're drunk, you're respectable."

Ákos smiled.

Later, as she was lying on the sofa in the connecting room, listening to Pista and Kati making love in the kitchen, she could think of nothing save for this smile.

Now that Eva was able to picture Ákos sitting at his desk, creating places and characters phrase by phrase, her interest in him and his writing had only grown. But Ákos's behaviour had also changed since that evening she took him home—

He had started talking to her (albeit with downcast eyes); he was often nearby and once even touched her forearm. Moreover, he hardly drank anything anymore, usually spending the entire evening with the same half-full glass in his hand. Then, two weeks after the evening that had changed everything, he told Eva he wanted to show her a book. Would she come over to his apartment for a short while?

Eva looked at him in surprise. Although Pista had asked her what had happened that evening, because Ákos had started talking about her with great frequency, she had not expected him to invite her over. Perhaps he really did only mean to show her a book; she had seen the piles of them on his desk. Maybe he had a copy of Kafka's *The Trial*, which was very difficult to get hold of. Or might he even give her his own novel to read?

This time his hand was twitchy as he unlocked the door to his room. He invited her in and offered her a glass of water. She declined and let him help her out of her coat, which he hung on a hook by the door.

As he removed his own coat, hanging it over hers, she stood in the middle of the room and wondered which of the books on the desk he was intending to show her. Suddenly she felt his hand on her side; he put his arm around her waist as if it were perfectly natural, as if it had always been there, all her life.

She turned around and looked at him in astonishment.

"What are you doing?" she asked, but he said nothing.

His eyes were lowered, staring at the floor, at the dark knots in the parquet. Each knot represents a severed branch, she thought. He remained perfectly silent, as if he had lost his voice.

But his body spoke, replacing the missing words. He pushed her onto the bed, onto the thin mattress. The bedspread had been freshly washed, smelling of lavender soap. Before she could roll away or get up again, one of his hands pressed her with all his might into the smell of lavender, while the other opened his belt, pulled his trousers down, and yanked up her tartan skirt.

Eleven years earlier, when the soldiers of the Red Army had overrun the country, rapes had been the order of the day. It was said that millions of women and girls had been raped during the advance westwards, fifty thousand in Budapest alone.

Eva knew some of these women, probably more than she thought, for nobody had spoken about it in Budapest. In the country, by contrast, women had discussed it openly, at least amongst themselves when there were no men about as they worked in the rice fields. They had cursed their rapists, fantasising about the most horrific ways in which they might die. Some also talked of how their perception changed while they were being raped. They had stepped out of their bodies and seen themselves from above as if they were floating on the ceiling. With Eva it was different. She lay beneath Ákos and was unable to leave her body. On the contrary, she was more painfully aware of it than ever before.

54.

When, one week later, on the evening of 23 October, two hundred thousand people assembled outside the parliament building, demanding freedom of expression and of the press, the reappointment of the deposed Imre Nagy as head of the government, and free elections, Eva lay on the sofa bed in the darkened connecting room, staring at the small picture of the Virgin Mary that hung beside the portrait of a fake great-uncle of hers. Since waking last week around midday, without being able to recall how she had left Ákos's room and made it home, she had not been able to shake off the idea that, with the lie about the divine child, Mary had hushed up a rape that would have robbed her of all honour without her having been to blame.

On the evening when János and other demonstrators had torn down and beheaded the statue of Stalin on Felvonulási tér, Eva had slept. Since the previous week she had spent most of the time asleep, only leaving the sofa to go to the lavatory. At first she was horrified by the dark, violet-blue mark that her pearl necklace had left on her skin, but now she had become used to her changed reflection.

She slept a lot without really being tired; the only point of it was to pass the time. Lajos brought her food in bed, for her family thought she had caught the flu or something similar. Her father would also sit with her for hours. He had lost his job with the post office because he had no longer been able to get out of bed in the mornings. Now he only left the apartment to buy cigarettes in the shop downstairs.

Even now, with the people rebelling against the regime, the dismembered Stalin statue being dragged through the streets, and the government giving the order to fire at the crowd of protestors outside the radio building, he stayed at home.

Before Pista left the apartment in the afternoon, they had argued about this. Pista accused him of being a coward and an opportunist who only ever came down on one side when victory was already certain. In one sense Pista was right: he was a coward and an opportunist, but this time it was not courage that was lacking; it was simply the energy to do the right thing.

Whereas on the evening of 23 October, Imre Nagy was still calling on the crowd outside parliament to go home, early the following morning he was, surprisingly, appointed prime minister by the central committee of the Hungarian Working People's Party. At the same time the unrest spread from Budapest to the whole of Hungary. Revolutionary committees, national councils, and workers' councils were formed and a nationwide general strike proclaimed.

János was a co-founder of one of the many new independent newspapers, and he urged Pista to write an article about the armed storming of the radio building, which he had taken part in, on 23 October.

Pista wrote the article in the smoke-filled atmosphere of the editorial office they had set up in the Cellar. Now he rarely showed his face at home, spending all of his time in the office, with revolutionary friends, or outside in the pulsating city.

Lilly and Lajos were terrified that something would happen to him, for fighting was still going on in the streets, but Eva was certain that he would come to no harm. Even when hundreds of peaceful demonstrators were shot dead outside parliament on 25 October, she was not worried that he might be one of them.

That same day party secretary Gerő, who had asked the Soviet Union for military reinforcements on the night of 23 October, was deposed and replaced by Kádár.

The fighting ended on 28 October when Nagy called for a ceasefire in a radio address. Eva was lying on the sofa bed in the darkened connecting room; her father was sitting on the wooden chair beside her. Nagy's voice filled the room. He described the rebellion as a "great, national democratic uprising, embracing and unifying all the people." Eva and Lajos avoided looking at each other; they were ashamed at not being part of this uprising, ashamed at their weakness and self-centredness, even though both of them knew that in their state there was no way they could be interested in the well-being of Hungary—they had to first sort themselves out before they could be of any help to their country.

On the morning of 4 November, only three days after Nagy had declared Hungary's neutrality and withdrawal from the Warsaw Pact, Eva woke with a start because the picture of the Virgin Mary fell to the floor. The water in the glass on the bedside table next to her quivered. She sat up, put the pillow behind her back, and switched on the radio—

The same voice which for the past few days had repeatedly cracked with excitement and joy about the news it had been able to announce now struck a serious and emphatic tone as it called upon the civilian population to take up arms for the new Hungary, for democracy, and for freedom.

Eva turned off the radio, threw back the blanket, set her feet on the wooden floor, stood up, went to the picture of the Virgin Mary, its glass cracked, and hung it back on the nail. Then she lay down again.

The Soviet Union invaded Hungary with two thousand tanks and two hundred thousand soldiers. Alarmed by the tanks, which were creeping through the city like huge primaeval woodlice, tearing up the tarmac with their tracks, Pista returned to the apartment for the first time in days.

As Lajos, to whom he refused to speak, was smoking out of the kitchen window, he sat on the sofa beside Eva. A dim grey light slanted through the roller shutters, which for a moment made his sister look like a corpse. She seemed to resemble her grandmother, who had drowned long before either of the two of them was born.

When Eva realised that it was Pista, not her father, sitting beside her, she opened her eyes and sat up. She could not stand the look of concern on her father's face or his solicitude, especially as he was not in a good way himself, which is why she sometimes pretended to be asleep.

Pista told her about the past few days, the masses of people in the streets, the new era, and the new Hungary which now had to be defended. He cursed the Russians who, as forward-looking as they were, had also confiscated their hunting rifles during the expropriation. He talked and talked, only stopping when Eva gently interrupted him.

"I was raped," she said.

Pista stared at her, and she could not have said what he was feeling.

As she looked at the picture of the Virgin Mary, it struck her that no feminist endeavour could achieve anything if men were stronger than women and could do something like that if they felt like it.

"By who?" Pista asked.

Eva said nothing.

Pista looked at his hands.

Church music carried to them through the open kitchen door.

"Did you know that Mama used to smoke too?" she asked.

Pista looked at her.

"It's why she doesn't allow you to smoke inside. She's worried she'll want to start again."

Pista shook his head.

"Who did it, Eva?"

She looked again at the picture of the Virgin Mary.

55.

For the next few days, without eating or sleeping, Pista roamed the streets of the city that had been plunged into chaos. He only spoke to people to ask after Ákos, whom nobody had seen since that evening a few weeks earlier. Pista was the only one who had been friends with him, the rest having at best tolerated his presence.

Ákos was not at home either. The widow who let the room refused to open the door for Pista, but did tell him that she had not seen Ákos for more than a week, and that he had not mentioned any upcoming trips or anything similar.

Pista nodded, thanked her for the information, and left the gloomy building. Ákos had gone to ground and nobody knew where. Not a single person seemed to know anything about him, and as Pista walked through the streets, ever wary of running into Soviet rifles, he realised that he barely knew Ákos either—

He knew neither where Ákos had grown up nor in what circumstances. From his surname he concluded that his family could possibly be the descendants of the imperial and royal court jewellers and, later, Viennese bankers. But he had no idea what work Ákos's father had done. Pista did not even know if he had siblings, for they had never spoken about things that related to their personal lives. What was the point of talking to each other about their lives in freedom when amongst the rats even the memory of these was unfamiliar?

The longer Pista wandered the streets, the more often he ducked into an entrance or threw himself on the ground behind a parked car, because he fancied he had seen a soldier in a window or behind a tree.

He had not slept for days, had prowled through the city from morning till evening in search of Ákos, and at night had lain awake with tired limbs, full of self-reproach. Every ten minutes he would get up, open the kitchen window, and puff cigarette smoke out into the silence of the night, which was from time to time interrupted by a gunshot. As Pista smoked, he imagined finding his friend, the young Petőfi, smashing his nose, gouging his eyes, knocking out his teeth, scratching his cheeks, mangling his ears, tearing out his hair, breaking his arms, legs, fingers, ribs, even toes, then throwing him into the Danube.

While he fantasised about Ákos's disfigured body, hid from imaginary soldiers, and could permanently hear the rumbling of the Russian tanks, he thought again of his great-uncle Imre, whom he had not seen since the expropriation. Now he believed he understood Imre, believed he knew what it was like to go mad, to lose your mind without being able to do anything to prevent it. He saw the soldiers in the windows aiming their rifles at him and threw himself on the ground, even though he knew they existed only in his mania.

He also thought about the time many years back when he had been able to talk to shadows, and when he was not yet afraid of this intermediate world into which he now slipped again after so long.

Several times a day Pista saw dead bodies. If they were lying facedown, he would roll them onto their backs to see if they were Ákos. Whereas he had almost thrown up at the sight of the first corpse, whose face resembled a wax mask, after three days he felt as if the dead bodies had always been part of the cityscape, as if corpses had lain on the pavements, in doorways, and in parks ever since he could recall.

As he walked past them, he wondered what work they had done, whom they had loved, and what they had believed in. Once he turned over the body of someone he knew, a former classmate who had not picked on him but had not protected him either. Pista had not seen him since the war. Now he was lying there before him, as a grown man—and yet was unmistakably the fifteen-year-old boy who had cheated in exams and been in love with Matilda's best friend, Eszter.

He was lying in front of a building with such a gaping hole in it that, as with the doll's house Eva once had, you could look into the rooms. Pista saw a green shower curtain and in the room beside it a brown-and-beige-striped carpet, and a bed that was covered in rubble but was otherwise intact. If you ignored the three gunshot wounds in his belly, it looked as if his former classmate had simply fallen out of this house.

Pista did not know what he was actually doing. He was looking for his sister's rapist while she lay in her tiny, darkened room in their tiny apartment, never having asked him to avenge her. What she had asked him to do was to stay. But he had not been able to do this. He had found it impossible to sit at her bedside in the knowledge that he was to blame for having failed to protect her.

So he wandered, wandered through the workers' outer districts, the parks, and the city centre, across the bridges and the hills on the Buda side. He walked through the entire city that once again looked as it had done after the war, and, as if by a miracle, nothing happened to him.

The Hungarian army handed out weapons to the civilian population who set up roadblocks, made Molotov cocktails, and painted pan lids to make them look like anti-tank mines. They knew how to defend themselves, had experience of house-to-house fighting—the war and the Siege of Budapest were not that long in the past—but they lacked munitions and the Soviet army was vastly superior. It was a hopeless fight—but they went on fighting.

His search was hopeless too; Pista knew this. If Ákos did not wish to be found, Pista would not find him. He was a stranger, even though Pista knew each of his movements, each of his facial expressions, and all his political, philosophical, and literary views. After all, they had not talked about anything else, only ever circled around these abstract subjects in the hope of eventually stumbling across some deeper truth. All those months underground they had only discussed Nietzsche, Dostoevsky, and Márai, avoiding anything private. Even later on, when they were no longer these pale, skinny, shaven-headed figures from the mine, they had continued in the same vein. Nonetheless Pista kept searching, for if he could not protect his sister, at least he had to avenge her.

56.

When Pista did eventually give up on 9 November, the Soviet troops had already regained control of the capital. The population was ordered to lay down their weapons. Imre Nagy took refuge in the Yugoslav embassy and resolutely announced that he would not step down from the office of prime minister. But the people, who only a few days earlier had thought a return to the situation before the revolution inconceivable, no longer believed that their prime minister's determination could prevent the Soviet Union from trampling over the new Hungary, democracy, and freedom.

On 11 November martial law was imposed nationwide. Now the Soviet Union embarked on the systematic persecution of the rebels. The following day the state-controlled press announced the formation of a new government under Kádár, officially declaring Nagy dismissed.

Fearful of being arrested, Pista moved to Kati's where he would not be found so quickly. He slept on the rug beside the bed that she shared with her sister and thought incessantly about Eva.

Whereas to begin with he had only contemplated how he might find Ákos and had blocked out every thought of Eva, now he tried to imagine what it must be like for her, lying there alone in the darkened connecting room, listening to Radio Free Europe talk about the promise of military assistance from the west, which was never at any point intended. What difference would it make to her if the capitalist west supported Hungary in the fight against communism if she was never going to leave that darkened room?

As he lay awake, listening to the breathing of Kati and her sister, he pictured Eva also lying awake at that moment, trying to find her way back to herself and the world.

After a while, Pista went back home. Although the arrests had not stopped, he missed Eva, missed his mother, and even missed his father. In those sleepless nights on Kati's rug he had realised how hard he was on his father. He had always insisted that Pista be strong, not show his feelings, but keep going, always looking forwards. And yet, unlike him, his father had not only lost his future with the expropriation but his entire identity—

All his life he had been somebody without having to do anything to make this happen. All his life people had looked up to him, respected and admired him—and then, overnight, he was a broken man, a postal worker, a nobody.

Pista suddenly felt sorry for his father. He imagined how, as a young boy, he must have expected just as much from life as Pista had, imagined how his father must have believed that everything would be fine and the world was just—to them at least.

On the way from Kati's to their apartment he decided he would embrace his father when he got home. The city centre was still a picture of devastation. The roads were wrecked, shop windows smashed, trams lay on their sides, and many buildings had human-sized holes in them, which it rained through.

Kati's family had decided to flee to America. Her father said that difficult times were around the corner even for those who did not openly confront the regime.

"Over the next few years merely wearing a pair of spectacles will be enough to be deported to Siberia as an intellectual enemy of the state," he had said.

Pista did not think it would get that bad, but he was already rueing having written the article about the storming of the radio building for János's revolutionary paper and, in the flush of victory, putting his real name beneath it.

The following morning, 22 November, Imre Nagy was arrested as he left the Yugoslav embassy, despite Kádár's guarantee of safety, and deported to Romania. Four days later, as Kádár gave a radio address explaining the reason for the arrest, Pista saw his father wipe a tear from his eye, even though he had never liked Nagy on account of his land reforms. Again Pista would have liked to embrace his father; again he left it.

While thousands took part in marches and memorial events for those who had been killed during the revolution, lit candles and laid wreaths on fresh graves, security officers in long black coats went from door to door. Countless people were arrested during these days.

When Pista said goodbye to Kati, he thought of Matilda; his leave-taking of her had been far more difficult. Sometimes, in moments like these, which ostensibly had nothing to do with Matilda, he would think of her and try to imagine what she would be like today. Usually he would be unsuccessful, but occasionally he would see her before him, crossing the road or entering a bakery.

On 11 December, one month after first imposing martial law, the government did it again in response to a general strike that left the whole of Budapest without electricity. As soon as the sun disappeared the streets were so dark that the men in long black coats could be identified only by the resounding clack of their hard boots.

All day long Pista stood at the open window, smoking and shivering from the cold, waiting for them to come to fetch him. But he was even more worried about János than himself; János would probably be hanged if he were arrested. He had not seen his best friend in more than two weeks. Pista had no idea where or how he was, not even if he was still a free man.

The men in long black coats roamed the city like hounds, wandering through all the streets and districts that Pista had searched on his hunt for Ákos, leaving boot prints in the fresh snow, which now also swallowed the sounds they made. And so János had no way of preparing for the ringing of his doorbell at six p.m. on 14 December; he was taken away in slippers and a vest.

57.

THE PSYCHIATRIC HOSPITAL LAY ON THE EDGE OF THE CITY IN a mansion that had belonged to a Jewish businessman who had died in the ghetto during the Second World War, and whose fortune had remained the property of the state after the Russian takeover of power. The area looked almost rural; the large, snow-covered gardens backed onto white fields that, for some time now, had repeatedly made Eva think of the bleak story of the blind man.

Imre sat at one of the tables in the deserted conservatory, gazing outside. For the past few weeks the sky had been a sea of grey, from which large flakes had come tumbling onto the city several times a day. Now the snowy fields beneath the white sun were so dazzling that you could barely look out. This did not seem to bother her great-uncle; he had turned not only his gaze but his whole body to the bright landscape through the wall of glass, while the reality inside did not appear to concern him.

It had not been easy to get permission for a visit to the hospital, but both of them were very keen to see Imre again.

Now that, five years later, they really were sitting opposite him and he met their gaze without any sign of recognition, it seemed like a mistake. They had come in the expectation of finding him unchanged (for how was his existence here any different from in the manor house?), but now he looked at them with vacant eyes, reminding them only on the surface of their great-uncle who had almost always been a part of their lives—at least on the margin of their field of vision, behind the window of the blue room.

Despite his venerable age, he had not lost his natural elegance, but otherwise was barely distinguishable from the other characters shuffling along the corridors of this house hour after hour, banging their heads, shaking, or muttering to themselves. He sat there as straight as a rod, motionless save for his left hand that did not seem to be part of his body but looked like a delicate, sinewy animal. It mechanically stroked the rough surface of the tablecloth, always in a circle.

The two siblings could not take their eyes off this hand. They sat there silently, all three of them, listening to the snow slide down the sloping glass roof of the conservatory, and to those individuals, lost and exiled in themselves, as they did their rounds, muttering to themselves all the while.

It then struck Pista, as he followed the circle of the hand, that perhaps Imre was looking at them with vacant eyes, not because *he* had changed, but because *they* were not the same people they had been five years earlier.

Snow trickled from the boughs of the trees that stood in the garden; the crystals shimmered in the clear air. Large white clouds had gathered in the sky, casting even larger shadows between which the snowy fields resembled ice floes in black water.

It was only seeing this that Eva realised how long she had lain behind the drawn curtains of the connecting room.

And only seeing this did Pista understand what it meant to be arrested by the men in long black coats.

János's arrest was two days ago. Two days underground. Two days of cigarette burns on the skin and electric shocks. Pista had also heard of cells where the prisoner could only stand or squat, sleep deprivation, and truncheon blows.

How long will he stick it out? he thought as the snow crystals trickled from the boughs.

How long will he remain silent? he thought as Imre described circles on the tablecloth.

* * *

When they got up, put on the coats they had hung over the backs of the chairs, wrapped the scarves around their necks, and slipped on their gloves, when they patted their great-uncle's shoulder again and gave him a final look before turning to go—he said, "Thanks for the lovely visit. It was very nice being with you."

They turned and looked at him in amazement, but he just sat there as before, with his vacant gaze and circling hand. All the same, they slipped off their gloves, unwrapped their scarves, hung their coats over the backs of the chairs, and sat down again.

Without looking at them, Imre now said, "You cannot stay much longer. You have to go before they come and it gets dark."

It was late morning and Pista had no idea who it was who might come—but as the snow continued to trickle from the boughs and Imre, who now could not stop talking, spoke of a hunting lodge in which people were waiting for him, Pista remembered the rustling of the forest in the evenings. The song of the blackbird. The cooing of the pigeon. The smell of the elderflower, its velvet white in the blue of dusk. He remembered the sheen of the blackberries, the shadows that turned ever darker. The light in Pontiller's window and the voice on the other side of his wall. The portraits and corridors, the staircases and the furniture, the China-red lampshades and the curtains in front of the open windows of the drawing room, the pattern on the blue carpet in the playroom, and the blue walls in Imre's room. Perhaps his flight into madness had been the only sensible move.

58.

When the train left the station, Lajos cautiously reached for Lilly's hand, as if he had long ago lost permission to do this—but rather than withdrawing her hand as he had expected, she left it in his until the train was no longer visible.

Eva and Pista travelled past white fields, small villages, forests, and the occasional rundown manor house where friends of their family had once lived and which now, like the mansion where Imre was housed, belonged to the state. In the distance, becoming lost in the haze, lay the mountains where fighting persisted.

Eva thought of Aunt Ilona, who eighteen years earlier had also boarded a train to leave their home. They had not seen each other since, the Bleichröders never having returned, and yet Eva knew every detail of their flight—

How often had her father got into a lather about his sister when yet again she wasted precious time during their telephone conversation across the ocean talking about this flight that everyone in the family already knew by heart!

"*That's* why they had to lay deep-sea cables thousands of kilometres long," her father would say with a shake of his head each time he hung up.

"Imagine we were on a train with Sándor Márai right now," Eva said, back in the present. "Then we'd have an escape story of our own to tell."

"He's already in exile," Pista said.

Eva nodded.

"That's true."

Then they fell silent until the train pulled into Pécs, trying to get used to the idea that they too would soon be exiles.

Following the first wave of refugees escaping Hungary, the border with Austria was now closely guarded, so they had decided to flee to Yugoslavia, from where they planned to go on to Switzerland. Unlike during the Second World War, Switzerland was now welcoming Hungarian refugees with open arms because, according to the weekly newsreels, Hungary, which had taken a stand against communism, had been "abandoned by the free world in its fight."

After lunch not far from the house where they had lived during the war, they climbed into a lorry full of potatoes, having given the driver the rest of their money to take them to the Yugoslav border.

As they sat amongst the sacks, both of them thought about their time on the farm and their parents, who had decided to remain in Budapest.

"We're too old for that sort of thing," her mother had said. "If Switzerland really is as beautiful as everyone says, we can always follow on later when the weather's a bit warmer."

"Besides, it would be a shame for us to leave again, now that you're finally going and we've got the apartment to ourselves," their father said with the grin that made him look like a schoolboy and which they had not seen for ages.

After they had sat in the dark for what must have been an hour, without saying anything, Pista asked, "Did you know that the Swiss haven't been at war for over a century?"

"Yes, but women aren't yet allowed to vote."

"Really? And you still want to go there?"

"I've heard the streets are very clean. And if you stand on the shore of Lake Zurich you can see the mountains at the end of it. At least that's what Sonia told me. She was there with her family some years ago."

When the lorry stopped and the driver let them out, the sun was just setting behind a nearby strip of woodland.

"You have to go through here," the driver said. "Through these woods until you get to a river. Once you've crossed that, you just need to climb the bank and you're in Yugoslavia."

"How are we supposed to cross the river?" Pista asked.

"That's not a problem. It's frozen solid and very shallow."

The dry snow crunched beneath their shoes as they crossed the field to the edge of the black wood. Each carried a leather rucksack. Inside were:

two jumpers
two photographs of their parents
a photo of the manor house
a pair of trousers
a skirt
underwear for three days
two passports
a knife
a loaf of bread
a torch

At the very bottom of Eva's rucksack was also the book she had been carrying around for years, which had been at the manor house, the city house, the farm, and in the tiny apartment in Budapest. Soon after Edmund's arrest she found it beneath his mattress and ever since had opened it whenever she felt lost or lonely.

This had often been the case over the past few weeks. And until Pista had returned from his hunt for Ákos, she thought it would always be thus, that she would never find her way out. But now that she was going step by step towards the woods, the sky above them getting darker and the frozen earth and hard snow crunching beneath their shoes, now that the cold of the coming night was slapping her in the face and she wondered whether sub-zero temperatures and a snowy landscape were part and parcel of a flight, whether a flight was somehow unthinkable without adverse climatic conditions, she felt in control of her own life again. This feeling was out of step with the reality of the situation. In truth she had probably never been less in charge of her destiny than during these hours.

No sooner had they reached the edge of the woods than they were blind. The sky, which still held the light of the day and reflected the brightness of the snow, was barely visible from beneath the densely growing trees. It was as if they were walking on the bottom of a very deep lake.

Sometimes the cry of a bird rang out through the wood, making them jump, or a twig in the undergrowth snapped noisily beneath their feet. They walked one in front of the other to lessen the chance of being spotted. Although the patrols were not as numerous as on the border with Austria, they did exist, and here they also risked being interned in a camp if they were caught. Or they might be shot on the spot, without ceremony or pity.

The woods were larger than they had thought, and their headway was slow. The snow, which here—where the wind that whistled across the fields could not reach it—was damper and deeper, made walking difficult, and the darkness hindered their progress. For fear of being discovered they left the torches in their rucksacks.

For more than two hours they trudged through the woods until the trees thinned abruptly, affording a view of the river. To give themselves an idea of the lie of the land and to avoid running straight into the rifles of Russian border guards, they squatted in the undergrowth by the edge of the woods and observed both sides of the river as best they could.

It was so quiet that Eva could hear her own breathing and Pista's heartbeat. To distract herself from the cold spreading through her limbs now that they were no longer moving but sitting tight in the vegetation as tensely as hunted hares, she turned her thoughts to the last few weeks which, in this unfamiliar landscape of black woodland and white snow, seemed like a dream from long ago. Even the deceit and the time before that, when she had almost fallen in love with Ákos, felt like incidents in a story somebody had told her or she had read somewhere.

"We need to keep going," Pista said after a while. "Who knows when the next patrol will come past."

Eva nodded. A river and a field, this and no more lay before them now. But what came afterwards, what lay beyond the river, beyond the field? Yugoslavia. Switzerland. Lake Zurich and at the end of it the white mountains.

She was able to imagine all of this; she had images of it and she had words for it. But she could not envisage herself in Switzerland, could not evoke herself in a country to which she had only had a connection through Imre, who more than half a century earlier had spent time there, somewhere in the white mountains, in a sanatorium.

Eva suddenly felt the uncontrollable urge to simply turn around, turn her back on the river, the future, and freedom, and take the train back to her familiar life. But Pista, who was entertaining the same thoughts, doggedly went on his way, and she followed without saying anything.

A fine layer of snow covered the ice on the river; it was impossible to tell how thick the ice was. When Pista tentatively placed a foot on it, he did not hear the crunch beneath the muffling powdery layer. He shifted his weight forwards, onto the foot on the ice—and broke through it with a gentle crack.

"What now?" Eva said.

"We have to get across nonetheless. The driver said it was shallow. Or we allow ourselves to be shot. We don't have any other options."

Before Eva could respond, he turned, stepped on the ice, broke through it, pulled a face, kept going, and tried not to scream with cold and fear. Eva followed him, stepping into the ankle-deep water that soon became knee-deep, and looked for support from the smoothed stones and the image of the white mountains at the end of Lake Zurich. It did not get any deeper; they waded through the river.

Once they got to the other side, they heard barking.

"Run!" Pista cried at once.

And then again: "Run, Eva! Run!"

Only then did she start running, up the riverbank, with sore feet and legs scratched by shards of ice. She fell, got back up, fell again, ignored the hard snow that scraped the palms of her hands and her cheeks, felt only her heart throbbing in her chest, beating and pounding.

Pista was a few metres ahead of her, already running across the field when she got to the top of the bank. Her feet and legs began to turn numb; the barking became quieter, Pista slower. He must not fail her again. But Eva kept running, kept running until she caught up with him and then was running alongside him, without thinking, without feeling, as if she had been made for it, to run away.

She ran until two soldiers stood in her way with rifles pointing at her, and her pounding heart fell out of her chest. It lay there in the snow, bloody and twitching like a fish.

59.

A HENHOUSE, JUST TALL ENOUGH TO STAND IN, A STAINED mattress, three counterpanes, two stoves, and a bare bulb—this was freedom for the time being.

The two soldiers who had intercepted them a week earlier had not been Russian but Yugoslavian. They had taken Eva and Pista—both of them half unconscious from the cold, tension, and exhaustion—to the nearest village, where Hungarian refugees were billeted in the local inn.

Although the inn was already so full that people were even sleeping in the corridors and they had been put in the henhouse behind the building, anything was better than ending up in the basement of the ÁVO or in a camp. Besides, here they were given hot tea, goulash soup, and warm clothes, donations that the Red Cross had brought in lorryloads from Switzerland to the Hungarian border.

At night it was freezing cold despite the stoves, which meant they had to snuggle up to each other as they used to on the farm. When five days later a second mattress was brought in and a young couple joined them in the henhouse, it became a little warmer.

The woman was pregnant and had such a craving for pickled cucumbers that her husband Lászlo spent his days traipsing around the village, exchanging his cigarettes for jars of gherkins. Pista helped him.

He took an immediate liking to Lászlo, and their forays through the snowy village took his mind off the men in long black coats, from whom he did not yet feel safe, not even here across the border, which after all was just a line on a map, an idea in people's heads, and in reality was nothing more than a narrow, shallow river.

Eva meanwhile spent hours talking to Nicolette, who after just a few days felt like a long-standing friend. Her optimism and humour were infectious, and Eva admired her courage to flee with an unborn child to a country where they knew nobody. They intended to go to Switzerland too, where the swans were said to be whiter than freshly washed linen.

60.

When they passed Zagreb, where the roofs were covered in snow and the chestnut trees bare, it occurred to Pista that this was where his parents had spent the only night of their honeymoon. Then his grandfather Sándor had fallen down the stairs and fractured his skull.

They had wanted to go to the sea and to Rome, but had only made it as far as Zagreb. He imagined them on this one evening strolling down the chestnut-lined streets, which they were passing now, more than three decades later, imagined them after dinner in a small restaurant, lying side by side on the hotel bed, listening to the sounds of the night through the open window, which if you listened as carefully as they did were subtly different from those in Budapest. He recalled the wedding photographs, his parents' faces, their shining eyes, their ornate clothing, and their hands, which in these pictures were always close to the other person.

How unbelievably young they had been then! Younger than he was now, younger even than Eva!

Nicolette had asked that morning whether she would be godmother to her child. Eva had nodded eagerly and cried for joy.

Now she was asleep—her head leaning against the window, through which the snowy roofs and streets flew past, her mouth half open, hands clenched—and she looked like a child.

Pista realised that he would never be able to protect her. All he could do was be there for her.

He looked at her until he sensed that she would wake up under his gaze. Then he stared outside again. White fields, black trees, the sky blue, and the occasional farm. Zagreb was behind them—and with it the entire world that they knew.

Before them lay Zurich, the lake, the white swans, and snow-covered mountains.